SECRETS

EXTREME CAUTION
by Jean Brashear

From the opening green flag at Daytona to the final checkered flag at Homestead, the competition will be fierce for the NASCAR Sprint Cup Series championship.

The **Grosso** family practically has engine oil in their veins. For them racing represents not just a way of life but a tradition that goes back to NASCAR's inception. Like all families, they also have a few skeletons to hide. What happens when someone peeks inside the closet becomes a matter that threatens to destroy them.

The **Murphys** have been supporting drivers in the pits for generations, despite a vendetta with the Grossos that's almost as old as NASCAR itself! But the Murphys have their own secrets... and a few indiscretions that could cost them everything.

The **Branches** are newcomers, and some would say upstarts. But as this affluent Texas family is further enmeshed in the world of NASCAR, they become just as embroiled in the intrigues on and off the track.

The **Motor Media Group** are the PR people responsible for the positive public perception of NASCAR's stars. They are the glue that repairs the damage. And more than anything, they feel the brunt of the backlash....

These NASCAR families have secrets to hide, and reputations to protect. This season will test them all.

Dear Reader,

When I was first invited to be part of this very cool NASCAR: SECRETS AND LEGENDS series, my reaction was "me?" What I knew about the sport could have danced on the head of a pin with lots of elbow room. But a little research got me intrigued and...well, to say I've become an avid fan (you do know that word comes from fanatic, right?) is an understatement.

I've watched endless hours on SPEED TV, sat through race after race, riveted, read NASCAR.com every day, will discuss racing at the drop of a hat with perfect strangers...I've got it bad. I attended my first race at Bristol—a thrill of a lifetime—and I'm eager to try every track on the circuit. (If you'll visit my Web site, www.jeanbrashear.com, you can see my photos.) People who've never gotten into NASCAR don't know what they're missing—it's a complex and fascinating sport.

So I'm thrilled to be a part of this series and excited to be writing two books for Harlequin's officially licensed NASCAR romance series in 2009, available in February and November of next year. I love to hear from readers via my Web site or www.eHarlequin.com. Thanks for coming along with me on this ride!

All my best,

Jean

NASCAR

EXTREME CAUTION

Jean Brashear

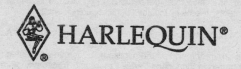

HARLEQUIN®

TORONTO • NEW YORK • LONDON
AMSTERDAM • PARIS • SYDNEY • HAMBURG
STOCKHOLM • ATHENS • TOKYO • MILAN • MADRID
PRAGUE • WARSAW • BUDAPEST • AUCKLAND

Recycling programs
for this product may
not exist in your area.

ISBN-13: 978-0-373-21798-4
ISBN-10: 0-373-21798-6

EXTREME CAUTION

Copyright © 2008 by Harlequin Books S.A.

Jean Brashear is acknowledged as the author of this work.

NASCAR® and the NASCAR Library Collection® are registered trade-
marks of the National Association for Stock Car Auto Racing, Inc.

www.eHarlequin.com

Printed in U.S.A.

JEAN BRASHEAR

Two-time RITA® Award finalist, *Romantic Times BOOKreviews* Series Storyteller of the Year and recipient of numerous other awards, Jean has always enjoyed the chance to learn something new while doing research for her books—but never has any subject swept her off her feet like NASCAR. Starting out as someone who wondered what could possibly be interesting about cars racing, she's become a die-hard fan, only too happy to tell anyone she meets how fascinating the world of NASCAR is. (For pictures of her racing adventures, visit www.jeanbrashear.com)

Acknowledgments

Mike Sobey, Gaylynn Sizemore and Quitman Liner were my first teachers in the world of racing, while Suzanne Brooks shared legal insights and Doak Fling helped me understand Maeve's financial options. Leah Sommerville and Pauline Spencer at Texas Motor Speedway—thanks so much for the fabulous tour! Thanks to Bob and Nancy Hart for letting me stay in your gorgeous lake house while I was at Bristol.

I owe more than I can possibly express here to Patsy and John Hart for hosting, driving, sweating during the brutal August heat with me…for so much that friendship shouldn't have to cover but did anyway. You made my time in Bristol absolutely terrific, and I will never forget the trip.

To Marsha Zinberg and Tina Colombo at Harlequin, thanks so much for inviting me to join the fun! Thanks to everyone at SPEED TV for taking me inside the world of NASCAR, teaching and entertaining me both. To the many people of NASCAR who make the races happen, for the thrills and chills you give us all, thank you from this new and die-hard fan.

And to all the lovely NASCAR fans I've met along the way, thank you for your kindness and generosity—let's go racin'!

REARVIEW MIRROR:

Despite the debacle Maeve Branch's life has become—her embezzler husband leaving her practically penniless, his secret mistress of twenty years penning a tell-all book and her family being spotlighted by scandal, those in the know are predicting that the elegant socialite will soon find a fresh start…and a second chance at love.

PROLOGUE

Dallas
Late August

MAEVE MACGREGOR BRANCH eagerly studied the television screen for a sight of her twin sons, Will and Bart, during the pre-race show for the NASCAR Sprint Cup Series night race at Bristol. She'd spoken with both of them earlier in the day, and she knew they were aware that she'd be watching them as she had every single race they'd driven since their go-kart days.

Until this season, though, she'd have been at the track with them, not in front of the TV. Nothing, however, was normal about their lives anymore. Never would be again. She couldn't bear knowing she was letting her children down.

But she just wasn't ready.

The shock of her husband's disappearance, the huge sums Hilton had embezzled from his company—her family's company, curse him—those were only the beginning.

His mistress of twenty years, Alyssa Ritchie, and her tell-all book accusing Maeve of being cold in bed and only out for the lifestyle Hilton had provided her with—oh, that was another stake in her heart, a humiliation she could barely stand to think about. Especially since there was no truth to it. Maeve came from money, and she'd been everything Hilton had wanted in a wife. Her family had given him his start in the world, and she'd never, *never* liked the high life she'd been forced to live to keep up appearances, something that was very important to him.

She'd handed him all she had—and he'd lied to her. About everything.

Then left her practically destitute.

But none of that compared to his worst sin. Hilton had hurt her children, her precious children, and she would never forgive him for that. They were his, too, yet he'd left them all high and dry. Penny, their eldest, had become a fashion model to please her beloved daddy, and she was devastated by his betrayal. Sawyer, their youngest, to whom Hilton gave money and things, instead of love, had been estranged from them all until recently.

And the twins, upon whom Hilton had placed his greatest ambitions and pumped up his own enormous ego, had been robbed of the sponsorships so critical to a NASCAR Sprint Cup Series team. Without those millions of dollars, Bart and Will, both such promising drivers, had faced having their careers cut short.

To say nothing of the firestorm of scandal and

disgrace that had been heaped upon the whole family. The tabloids had been having a field day since Daytona.

She was proud of her children for pulling together, for not giving up when the future had seemed so dark. She was trying to do the same herself. Desperate but determined to succeed in rising from the ashes of the life she'd once thought perfect.

But she wasn't doing nearly as well as her children were, and that shamed her.

She returned her attention to the screen, remembering how exciting this race had always been, how much she'd enjoyed traveling to beautiful East Tennessee. The hottest ticket in NASCAR, the Bristol night race was called, and in all the races she'd attended, she had to agree that there was nothing like it. Screaming fans and forty-three roaring engines packed inside what was basically a coliseum, one the Roman circus could only have dreamed of being in. A wall of sound, literally. She'd swear there was not one molecule of empty air. The lights, the spectacle… She got shivers even now, just thinking how her blood started pumping long before the heralded cry: *Gentlemen, start your engines!*

In the past, she'd been there at the track and loved every minute of being with her boys, however little she'd ever imagined, in her privileged, protected childhood in Dallas, that she'd ever be a part of something like NASCAR. Her father would have had a fit—he'd raised her to be the perfect society princess, however much the role had chafed her.

If she'd ever given NASCAR a thought, she would have assumed, as the uninitiated do, that stock car racing was an odd sport consisting simply of cars going round a race track.

The world she'd found was, instead, something very special. Fans ranged over the spectrum of society and from all ages, and the sport itself was a complicated mix of strategy, courage, skill and, above all, teamwork. NASCAR was a family, and she'd loved being a part of it. Though Hilton had insisted that they have household help for appearance's sake, Maeve loved to cook, and she'd sneak away, spending time in each of her sons' motor homes, cooking tasty and nutritious meals not only for them but sometimes for their teams and owners, even their fellow drivers. She'd been basically shy since childhood, and home and family had always been everything to her, all she'd ever wanted. She had been in her element inside that protected little world.

Hilton had stolen all that from her. He'd not only made her a laughingstock in Dallas society, but he'd made her a figure of pity in NASCAR circles. Many in Dallas had taken pleasure in the juicy gossip, but she'd received caring messages from many of her NASCAR friends. She would never forget them.

But she couldn't face them yet. Couldn't bear the pitying glances, however kindly meant.

She had to find her own way first. Had to figure out what her life would be from here on. She'd been a fool and trusted unwisely, but she would not make that mistake again. She would emerge from this disaster—somehow. She didn't want to feel defeated anymore. Didn't want to lean on her children again.

But she was frightened. Terrified she wouldn't make it.

Tonight, however, her only concern was her boys. Though she wasn't there with them, she would be watching every second.

As the engines fired up, she remembered the throaty roar, how she felt it through her whole body. She closed her eyes for a second and thought about the crowd, the excitement, the thrill of being a part of NASCAR, how it got in your blood and you were never the same again.

She said a fervent prayer for the boys—her sons, yes, but also all the teams, the drivers, the NASCAR officials, everyone down there on the track who was a part of the spectacle and magic that is NASCAR. *Keep them safe,* she pleaded, *every single one.*

Then a small smile curved her lips. She hadn't had a reason to smile in a long time.

And if You can see your way clear, Lord, let Will and Bart run just a little bit better than the rest.

The pace car moved out onto the track, the double line of cars following them, Will on the pole and Bart three rows back in seventh.

Maeve clasped her hands and bent forward in her chair, letting the excitement build, taking her away from the hurdles she had to face, letting her remember better days. She waited, along with millions of others, for the rallying cry that sent hearts flying as the flag dropped.

CHAPTER ONE

One month later

THE WOMAN KNOWN as Margaret to her fellow volunteers at the animal shelter stepped out of her ex-housekeeper Gerty's serviceable sedan in the shelter's caliche parking lot.

And out of her real life, the one where reporters and gossipmongers waited for her to emerge in public, to gauge her reaction to the fact that Hilton had been caught in the Bahamas and was now sitting in jail, watched for her to crumble so more dirt could be dished. Tongues could wag.

Here, the only tongues she came in contact with wanted to bestow doggie kisses. The only thing that wagged were canine tails. This place had long been her refuge, the one thing she did for herself. As a child, she'd dreamed of becoming a veterinarian, a goal that had scandalized her father. Not a MacGregor, no. The MacGregors were Texas royalty. A MacGregor, with a lineage going back to Stephen F. Austin's original colony that settled in Texas, did not wear blue jeans or clean up after animals.

But cats and dogs didn't lie to you. Didn't cheat. They lived in the moment and accepted what was. Didn't spend time questioning everything.

HER LAST JOB of the day was her favorite: walking Harry, an aging yellow Lab. "Hey, fella," she crooned as she approached him. His rheumy eyes looked up at her with hope, his tail slowly beating a tattoo on the side of his cage. "How's my boy today? You ready for a walk?" The poor dog broke her heart, as so many of them did.

"Why do you do it, Mom?" Penny had asked her more than once when she'd returned home, shaken by how callous her fellow humans could be about the fate of innocent creatures that couldn't speak for themselves. Only her children and Gerty knew about this particular volunteer work, and none of them understood why she put herself through it.

"They need me," was the only answer she'd come up with. Even before her world fell apart, this had been the most meaningful part of her week. She hadn't missed a single time—with the exception of those terrible weeks right after the scandal had broken.

Thank goodness Penny's husband, Craig, had, in his own kind way, bullied her into returning long before she was ready to face the world.

"You don't care what the papers say, do you,

Harry?" She crouched before him, scratching behind his ears as Harry groaned in bliss. "You're my guy," she crooned.

A long slurp of the tongue had her giggling. "Come on," she said, rising. "Let's go outside and you can water some trees."

Harry's ears perked up at the magic word *outside*.

Maeve held the leash and led him down the hallway between the cages, too intent on talking to Harry to notice the tall man who stood in the doorway, frowning.

"MR. LAWRENCE?" The manager of the animal shelter, Carolyn Mason, glanced behind her. "If you'd come this way, I'll show you the wing we hope to expand if the fund-raising drive is successful."

Chuck Lawrence yanked his gaze from the small woman who'd brushed past without looking up. Something about her seemed oddly familiar, but he couldn't pinpoint it.

"...would take an interest," Ms. Mason was saying. "Don't you agree?"

"I'm sorry. What did you say?"

A line formed between the woman's brows, but she smiled even more brightly. "I said that our organization would be so fortunate if more board members were like you and came to look at what we need to do our jobs."

For his part, he thought anyone who took a

position on a board of directors owed at least that much service, though he expected more of himself. He'd let himself be talked into this position by Cecily Dunstan, the woman he'd been dating for several months, though he had little patience with the do-gooder facade worn by too many social climbers with little or no interest in the actual cause.

"I couldn't agree more," he responded. If Chuck Lawrence made a commitment, he honored it. Just as he'd honored his wedding vows for years after his beloved late wife, June, was gone. He hadn't been able to face the dating scene and had chosen to redouble his efforts at making money, instead.

But he already had plenty of money—not because anybody handed it to him, but through backbreaking work as an oil-field roughneck coupled with the cunning bred into him by the grandparents who'd raised him. The thrill of making more was long since gone. In time, though, he'd turned his efforts to making a difference, to applying his funds where they could do the most good. His two sons and a daughter were grown and they'd inherit a nice nest egg when he was gone, but he believed that children handed wealth often did not turn out well, so he'd insisted that they make their own way thus far. They'd made him proud, every one of them, and though they all had their separate lives, they were a close family still, even if the heart of them, their mother, was gone.

"Mr. Lawrence?"

"Chuck. Call me Chuck." He wielded a lot of power, yes, first as an oilman and now as a venture capitalist, but he'd spent enough of his life at the bottom of the ladder that he understood the difference between social status and true worth as a human being.

"Certainly, Mr....uh, Chuck." She smiled. "Let's move outside for a minute. It's a little hard to hear over all the barking. The dogs get excited when a stranger arrives."

He glanced around him and saw with approval that though the shelter was crowded, the cages were clean and each animal had food and water. "You run a tight ship, it appears." He followed her through the doorway that opened onto a wide, grassy area.

"Without our volunteers, I don't know how we'd manage. We're seriously understaffed, yet another reason for the fund drive." At the sound of one dog's joyous barking, she smiled and turned. "Like our Margaret there. She's our special angel. Been coming here for several years every single week."

Chuck followed the pointing of her finger and saw the woman who'd passed him earlier. He couldn't help smiling, too. The yellow Lab who'd lumbered by him had seemed ancient, yet he was cavorting with the volunteer like a puppy. "Who is she?"

"Let me introduce you. She's wonderful. Margaret!" she called, and waved the woman over. "I have someone I'd like you to meet."

The volunteer shaded her eyes with one hand. "Could it wait?" she called. "Harry hasn't had his walk."

"She's very shy," the manager said. "Spends her time with the animals almost exclusively." She raised her voice. "Just for a second. I can ask Leo to walk Harry."

The woman's reluctance was clear. "Never mind," Chuck began. "Let's go on."

But as he was saying that, the woman and the Lab began to approach. Once again, something niggled at him, a sense of recognition he couldn't credit. He watched the woman closely as she neared. Probably five-four or -five, slim, clad in old blue jeans, a wrinkled cotton shirt and worn athletic shoes, her hair covered with a bandanna, she was probably younger than his fifty-seven, but not a young woman.

A few feet away, however, he thought he heard her emit a small gasp, quickly muffled. She ducked her head as Carolyn Mason introduced them. "Margaret MacGregor, this is one of our board members, Mr. Charles Lawrence."

"Chuck," he amended, and put out his hand. "Glad to meet you, Margaret. Carolyn here's been singing your praises."

"My pleasure," she mumbled as she shook his hand and just as quickly released him. "I'd better go now." With a tug of the Lab's leash, she all but ran away.

"I am so sorry," Carolyn said, confused.

"No big deal," Chuck responded absently, his mind engaged in recalling the brief glimpse he'd had of the woman's face. No makeup, not even lipstick, graced her features, but there was something... "MacGregor, did you say?"

"Yes, why? Do you know her?"

Do I? He couldn't shake the notion that he'd met this woman before, but where could that have been? Her hands had been soft and smooth, the hands of a woman with frequent manicures, not those of someone who performed manual labor. Her carriage, even with head bowed, was dignified, at odds with her rough attire.

He stared after her, wondering.

"Do you want me to call her back?" The anxiety in the manager's voice conveyed her concern that an influential board member might be put off, something the shelter clearly couldn't afford.

He shook himself. Focused on the manager. "No. No, that's fine. Now, where were we?"

The tour continued, with Chuck doing his best to return his attention to the matter at hand.

DEAR MERCY. Maeve's heart pounded double-time. *Don't panic. Maybe he didn't recognize you.* She rounded the corner of the building and forced herself to slow. "I'm sorry, Harry." She crouched before him, wrapping one arm around his neck. "I didn't mean to rush you, I just—" She dropped her head to rest it on his neck. "What am I going to do?" Despair swamped her. The shelter had been her one refuge, the lone escape from the prison her home had become. If that man…what was his name? He'd been a guest at one of the dinner parties Hilton had insisted on throwing when he wanted to lure new investors into some venture.

How she'd dreaded those command performances where she'd had to be the elegant hostess, where Hilton wouldn't leave a single detail alone, never mind that she'd learned social graces from birth while he'd grown up a factory worker's son. He'd pick at her choices until she wanted to scream, but she never did.

It was part of the devil's bargain she'd made, she saw now. She had never liked the glare of publicity, had only endured it to keep peace in the family. Her philandering husband, the fugitive embezzler, had demanded that she take her place in society, just as her father once had. If she'd known Hilton would turn out so much like her father, she wouldn't have married him.

But when she'd met the charming and handsome Hilton Branch, he'd seemed like the answer to a prayer. Her elder brother, her father's shining hope to succeed him in the family bank, had been killed in Vietnam, and her father had turned the glare of his ambitions on her, regardless of how ill-suited she was to the task. Hilton was so dashing and magnetic, so full of ambitions to be everything she was not. When he'd pursued her, she'd been dazzled. He'd supported her dream to make a home and raise a family, if not her wish to be a vet. He'd been a wizard with her parents, and she'd gratefully accepted his proposal, knowing that she'd provided her father with the heir she could never be.

If only her father hadn't died and Hilton's ambitions hadn't mushroomed. His new vision for a financial empire had him insisting on her playing a major role. He had no pedigree in society, and he needed her help to make those all-important connections.

She'd said yes, of course, eager to keep the peace. Only one of her many mistakes when it came to Hilton Branch.

Now the past she sought refuge from had returned to haunt her—in the one place she'd felt safe.

Lawrence. Charles Lawrence, that was his name. A wealthy oilman, she thought. His connection to Hilton made him loathsome to her. And dangerous.

Please, oh, please, let him not have recognized me.

If she lost this one piece of the week when she could forget the mess her life was in, she didn't know what she would do.

Harry whimpered and licked her hand.

Maeve's heart melted. "Thank you, my friend." She hugged him hard, then rose and straightened.

"Mom, you have to face them all down," Will had said to her recently. "Remember what you've always told us, never let them see you sweat."

An excellent strategy both he and Bart had had to master to succeed as they had in stock car racing. She was proud of her boys, she absolutely was. But they couldn't possibly understand. Neither of them had a timid bone in their bodies. She'd grown up scared of her shadow. Sought shelter in Hilton's.

Hilton Branch is out of your life now, Maeve Margaret MacGregor, and you had the wherewithal to raise four bright, strong children. God knows their father had little time to spare for them except when they occupied the limelight.

It was true. She had been the one to dry the tears, help with the homework, guide them into adulthood. She'd done a good job of it, too, if she did say so herself. Of all the mistakes she'd made—turning control of her life and their finances to Hilton Branch—raising fine children had not been among them.

If only she could manage to turn herself into a woman who could manage as well as her children did. The task seemed like the rest of her life: overwhelming.

Harry leaned against her leg, and she bent to pet him, wishing she could always have someone who loved her this much by her side.

Maeve stared at the old dog. In all the years she'd volunteered at the shelter, she'd never taken a single animal home, primarily because there were so many of them that it was impossible to choose, but also because Hilton had refused to have an animal in his house.

His house. *Her* house now—at least it was until she couldn't manage the upkeep anymore. Thank God it was paid for and couldn't be seized by creditors under Texas law, but all their other assets were still frozen except one, a trust fund set up for her many years ago by her father, money she'd meant to keep for her own grandchildren.

It wouldn't last forever, and she'd have to give up another piece of her past, but not yet. Not just yet.

She hunkered down. "Would you like to come home with me, Harry?"

A slurp over her jaw was his answer.

"Good," she said. "Good." Her former housekeeper, Gerty, would have a fit, but Gerty was supposed to be retired, anyway. Maeve couldn't pay her, but Gerty, loyal friend that she was, still showed up nearly every day on one pretense or another. Mostly because Gerty was worried sick about her, Maeve knew.

But now Maeve wouldn't be alone. In that moment, she let herself feel the terror she'd barely held at bay for months now, ever since that horrible day her world had crumbled.

She tightened her grip on Harry. "I am going to make it," she practiced saying. "I am going to make it."

If she uttered the words often enough, perhaps she would come to believe them.

"Come on, boy," she said to the dog. "My shift is over. Surely that man is gone now. Let's go fill out the adoption paperwork and head home."

Home. For the first time since her children had taken up their independent lives, Maeve had someone to care for. She couldn't wait.

She made it through the paperwork with a heart made lighter by Harry's presence. Of course she knew he wouldn't last forever. He was an old dog. But she could make the rest of his life comfortable, and she wanted to, desperately.

Her children had their own lives, their own burdens. It was time for them to stop worrying about her.

With a lighter step, she left the shelter with Harry by her side. She even chuckled a little, picturing Gerty's face when she found out that an old dog had ridden in her spanking-clean car.

She was still smiling as she rounded the car, making a list in her head of the supplies she would need. She was so busy she didn't hear the voice at first.

"Maeve? Maeve Branch?"

Her head whipped around to see Charles Lawrence observing her from a few feet away.

"Chuck Lawrence," he prompted. "We've met."

"Go away." Terror swamped her. "Please…go. I can't…" Her voice failed her.

"I mean you no harm."

The pity in his eyes made her stomach burn. "Please." Barely a whisper now. "Please…just let me be."

She jumped into her car and drove away as though demons were hot on her tail.

CHAPTER TWO

CHUCK STARED after her. He wasn't accustomed to frightening women, but apparently that was just what he'd done, intentionally or not.

He had plenty of commitments clamoring for his time. He didn't need to take on a basket case like Maeve Branch.

But he found himself intrigued. He'd met her in person only once before, at a dinner hosted by her insufferable blowhard of a husband, but she was hardly a stranger to him. Maeve MacGregor Branch. She came from one of the founding families of Texas, and her picture had been in the society pages often, at one charity ball or another or as a board member for various foundations, just as he was for this shelter. She'd always been a dignified, elegant figure, dressed to the nines and appearing coolly reserved, a clear case of *Do not touch. You are beneath me.*

At least, that was what he'd thought.

But the woman he'd heard about, the one he'd met at a dinner party, would never in a million years have donned old jeans and sneakers or cleaned up dog manure.

That woman wouldn't have laid one perfectly manicured finger on a broken-down old dog, much less taken him home.

Yes, her circumstances had changed radically—though, to be honest, he believed her far better off without the arrogant windbag she'd married. She might not think so, though—word around town was that she could barely pay the electricity bill.

So why, in those desperate straits, would she be volunteering her time when she probably needed a job, and pronto? What job skills could she have, though, coming from such a pampered existence?

And why was she working here under an assumed name? He frowned as he recalled that the manager had said "Margaret" had been coming here weekly for several years, not just since the scandal broke.

Obviously there was more to Maeve Branch than he—or anyone else, for that matter—had suspected.

Abruptly he wondered if what he'd taken for icy reserve might have been something else. The woman he'd encountered today had been both timid and frightened.

Except that she apparently had the wherewithal to tackle the full-time care of a broken-down dog.

Chuck had never been a man to leave a mystery alone, and this woman was definitely an enigma. He'd let her go as she'd begged him to, but he wasn't sure he could allow the matter to drop.

The gossipmongers had had a field day with the Branch scandal, and everything was stirred up again when Hilton was finally apprehended after being on the run for months. Maeve seemed to have few friends to support her. He'd always championed the underdog, probably because he'd been one himself for a lot of years. Now he liked to extend a helping hand to those who were exerting the effort to change their circumstances, just as he once had.

Maeve Branch might deserve what had happened to her, for all he knew, but something about her had touched him. He would do a little investigating and see what he turned up.

FOCUS ON YOUR DRIVING, Maeve thought. *Stop shaking.*

But it was hard, so very hard. That man, that Charles Lawrence—he'd ruined everything.

Chuck, he'd called himself, all friendly. *I mean you no harm.*

He did, though, she bet. Being in business with Hilton, part of the big-money crowd Hilton relished, how could he be any different from all the others who'd taken such pleasure in her downfall? Supposed friends like Liddy Caperton, whom she'd known since third grade at Hockaday, whose voice had dripped pity while her eyes danced with glee when she'd asked in that unctuous voice, "Whatever will you do now, Maeve? What a simply horrid surprise this must be, the mistress, the money… Oh, and Hilton's still a fugitive?"

The phone lines in the Park Cities had been burning for months now, quieting only briefly until something like Hilton's apprehension and arrest a few weeks ago lit them up again.

She'd learned who her friends were, that they were few in number, the price she'd paid for focusing so intently on her children and preferring to stay at home whenever possible. She understood now just how many of the so-called friendships had been predicated on her money and social position.

Her true allies had turned up in surprising places. Her hairdresser, Bobbie, who'd contacted Penny to volunteer to come to the house when Maeve couldn't bear to leave. Her elderly neighbor, Gladys Carpenter, whose bloodlines ran as deep in Texas history as Maeve's own and who touted Maeve's kindness when all Maeve had done was provide her with homemade pies and cookies now and again and share gardening tips over the fence.

And Maeve's beloved Gerty, who'd always had her back. Nothing on this earth would prevent her from being by Maeve's side in a crisis.

Her children, too, were a blessing. How lucky she was to have them. Their roles had seemed to reverse when Hilton wrecked their lives—Maeve's kids had been mothering her, but it was high time they returned to their lives and building their futures.

She was going to get her own life back together. If only she could figure out exactly how to do that.

Maeve hit the remote button to open the gate to

her estate. "We're home, Harry. At last, someone to appreciate the grounds I've spent years nurturing. They don't look so great now, since I had to let Alonzo go, but I'm enjoying digging in the dirt, and I'll like having you there with me, boy."

Harry plopped his head on her shoulder and groaned.

Maeve smiled and pulled into the garage. "There's just one little hurdle left, my friend." She smiled, thinking of how her children wondered aloud at times who was the true mistress of the house, Maeve or Gerty. "She'll grow to love you as I do."

I hope.

The door from the utility room opened. "About time you got home—" The words stopped on a near shriek. "What on earth is that?"

Maeve smiled at the diminutive woman in the doorway, the only member of the family smaller than herself—well, at least, until her newest companion. "Harry, meet my friend Gerty. You're going to be very happy here."

"What in heaven's name have you done? You're not planning to bring that beast inside, are you?"

Gerty had always been more bark than bite, and Maeve trusted the goodness in her. She decided that only the truth would serve. "My cover's blown at the shelter, Gerty. I don't think I can go back. This poor guy needs me," she continued. "And I need him."

Gerty's bluster died right then. "Oh, honey." She stepped aside and opened the door wide. "Bring him on in—" she shook a finger "—but go straight to the backyard. I will not have that creature muddying up the carpets. I'll gather towels and soap, then join you. You—" she pointed at Harry "—will bathe before you enter. You smell like a dog."

Maeve relaxed. "He *is* a dog, Gerty."

"Doesn't mean he has to smell like one. Leave it to me."

As Maeve passed her, Gerty squeezed her shoulder. "As for you, I have soup simmering, and you will eat every bit of what I give you. You're getting too thin."

"Oh, Gerty." Maeve blinked back tears. "What on earth would I do without you?"

"Humph," Gerty blustered. "As if you could. Now get on with you."

Maeve mustered a smile, feeling stronger just being home. Then she spied the stack of new bills on the kitchen counter and faltered.

Wondering just how much longer she would be able to hold on to her home.

HARRY SUFFERED through his bath in silent, wounded dignity. Lacking a proper tub Gerty was willing to let him into, the two women bathed him on the patio, using a garden hose. He was subjected to two shampoos with something fruity Gerty had nabbed from a guest bathroom, then toweled and rubbed for what seemed like hours before he met Gerty's standards for entry into the house.

Maeve left him with Gerty while she set up food and water for him and was just pondering where to make him a bed when she heard a screech and raced to the patio—just in time to see Harry rolling in the grass.

"You get back here, you…" What followed was a series of German curses Maeve chose not to understand, though she had learned a smattering from Gerty over her years as part of the household. "That's it! No inside for you." Gerty stomped past Maeve, her brow a thundercloud.

Maeve smothered a grin, all too aware from her years at the shelter that Harry's behavior was absolutely normal for a dog. But as soon as the door slammed behind Gerty, Maeve broke into giggles and collapsed on the grass. Harry came racing to her, tail wagging, tongue lolling as he proffered a wide doggy grin.

"Come here, you big oaf," she said fondly, and gave him a thorough petting. Harry used his bulk to lean into her and toppled her backward, then slurped his thanks on her cheek.

Maeve lay there in the grass, dappled sunlight playing over her body, and laughed until her stomach hurt.

When at last she fell silent, Harry settled next to her, his warmth along her side. Maeve kept her arm around his neck and sighed deeply.

And for the first time in many weeks, fell into a dreamless sleep.

GERTY GAZED through the kitchen window and shook her head. "Poor dear," she said as she watched the woman whose suffering she'd give a lot to vanquish.

Then her gaze fell on the dog, bits of grass and leaves stuck in the fur she'd worked so hard to clean.

"Good boy," she said with a smile. And picked up the phone to dial. "Penny," she said when it was answered. "Something upsetting happened to your mother at the shelter." Then she glanced back at the dog. "But I think the news is not all bad. Come see what your mother brought home."

LATE THAT NIGHT, Chuck Lawrence sat in his study, staring at the computer screen. How much information could be obtained by the simple click of a mouse never failed to astonish him. The world was a very different place from what it was when he'd first entered the business world, and light-years from the time he'd begun working in the oil fields.

He suspected Maeve Branch would be more than astonished. More like disheartened and possibly devastated. Her life lay there before him on the screen.

He could have hired a private investigator or assigned someone on his staff to do this search, but he hadn't, and now he was glad. He understood far better now why Maeve had been so terrified that she'd abandoned all her elegant manners and run from him. Every little salacious detail of her life had been picked over by magazines from *Newsweek* to *Sports Illustrated* to the corner gossip rag. Blogs on the Internet couldn't get enough of the Branch-family scandal, involving, as it did, one stunning supermodel, twin NASCAR stars, an ex-mistress making the rounds of the talk shows flogging her tell-all book. Juicy tidbits abounded everywhere he looked.

He'd even read some excerpts of that book online and experienced an urge to burn copies of it himself. He didn't believe half of what the woman had alleged, but plenty of people would. He tried to imagine what Maeve must feel like, having her children stalked by paparazzi, learning that her husband had cheated on her for twenty years, having not only her sex life—or sexual inadequacies, if Alyssa Ritchie was to be believed—exposed to the voracious gaze of voyeurs, but also far too many details of her financial straits heralded in reputable publications.

And dire straits they were. From what he could tell, Hilton Branch had lived far beyond his means, supporting not only a family but a mistress with exorbitant tastes while funding not one but both of his sons' NASCAR teams. One team's annual expenses could easily reach twenty million dollars, he'd read, and coupled with all the other excesses, Hilton had been robbing Peter to pay Paul for years—while apparently diverting many more funds into offshore accounts. When his house of cards had begun to topple, he and his money had vanished, leaving Maeve and her children all but destitute.

And recently, she'd lost her financial advisors—

likely, he guessed, because the picture was coming clear, now that Hilton had been found and arrested, that the money was gone and she would not be able to pay them.

None of which was, of course, his problem.

Except that he couldn't seem to forget how he'd put fear into Maeve's big violet eyes.

His plate was full, and he'd committed to plenty of causes that needed his help, like the wing he was thinking of donating to the animal shelter. He didn't need another underdog to champion.

And this one certainly hadn't asked him to. *Please…go.*

Chuck rubbed his hands over his eyes and stretched, weary after a very long day.

Then he rose and headed for bed.

He could call her, at least. Apologize for alarming her. Offer…what? *Please…just let me be.*

He would, if she insisted.

But the underdog he'd once been couldn't ignore a woman in such peril. Not without at least one attempt to let her know that not everyone was enjoying the debacle her life had become.

CHAPTER THREE

"MOM? ARE YOU in here?"

Maeve glanced up from the chaise in the sunroom and felt for the bookmark on the table beside her. "Penny, how are you, darling?" It was so good to see her daughter happy again now that she and Craig had mended their marriage.

Tall, blond and stunning, the only resemblance to her mother the violet eyes, Penny Branch Lockhart hurried to her mother's side with the grace she'd possessed long before she'd ever stepped onto a catwalk in New York or Milan. "I'm fine." She barely paused for breath. "But how are you?"

The worry in Penny's eyes was a dead giveaway. "Gerty called you."

"She loves you, Mom, as we all do. Tell me what happened at the shelter yesterday."

Just then, Harry groaned and rolled over, tail slapping the floor.

Penny blinked. "What is that?"

"Sweetheart, I'm almost certain love has not literally blinded you. That's a dog. My dog, to be precise."

Slowly, Harry rose to sitting, dropping his head on Maeve's legs.

Maeve smiled and stroked him. "Harry, meet my daughter, Penny." Then mischief took over. "Your sister, I suppose."

Penny reared back. "Mom!" Then she leaned forward and held out her hand for Harry to sniff.

Harry promptly made one long swipe with his tongue across her fingers. Maeve waited to see how her daughter would react.

"Oh, if you are not the sweetest thing," Penny crooned as she rubbed behind one ear.

"He really is," Maeve agreed.

Penny glanced over at her. "I can't remember the last time I saw you really smile. If Harry is the reason, then I'll gladly claim him as family."

Maeve sobered. "I have been a trial to you, haven't I, darling? You and Craig—all you children, really, but especially the two of you—have borne too great a burden. I never wanted that."

"Mom, you had your world shattered. Everything you believed true turned out to be a lie. Anyone would be devastated."

"But I'm your mother. I'm supposed to take care of you."

Penny laid her hand over Maeve's. "I'm thirty-two. All grown up."

"And beautifully so, but you've endured worse blows than I have." Just thinking about how desperately Penny wanted children and would never be able to bear one made Maeve so very sad. It had been the primary reason Penny had separated from Craig; he'd wanted a houseful of babies. It was so hard to see your child hurting, and though Craig and Penny had reconciled, that wound was slow to heal.

Penny's eyes darkened for a split second. Then she pressed her lips together, a telltale sign she was hiding something.

"What?" Maeve prompted. "Is something wrong?"

Penny shook her head, hesitating. Then she gripped Maeve's hands tightly. "I wasn't going to say anything until we were certain." Once more she hesitated. "But I can't stand it. Mom—" tears threatened, but her face split in a wide grin "—we may have found our baby."

Maeve gasped. "Oh, darling. I had no idea."

"We hadn't told anyone yet because the wait can take forever, but we've done all the paperwork and been approved by a wonderful agency in Fort Worth that's associated with a home for pregnant teens. Some people have to wait for years, so we didn't think…" The tears spilled over. "They've matched us with a young girl, and we're going to meet her next week. I'm excited and nervous and afraid to believe, but we might actually have a family, after all."

Maeve gathered her daughter close. "Honey, there is no justice in the world if two people as loving as you and Craig aren't considered perfect parent material." She squeezed her daughter and pressed a kiss to her hair. "Sweetheart, if there's a single thing on this earth I can do to help you, just say the word."

Then the thought hit her, and her eyes widened. "Oh, my. Baby shopping! And I'll knit. I haven't knitted in years, but I can't wait to get started."

Penny lifted her head from her mother's shoulder. "You would go shopping with me?" Both of them were all too aware that except for the visits to the shelter, Maeve hardly left the house. Thanks to the Internet and the collusion of Gerty and her children, she seldom had to. But at one time Maeve and Penny had delighted in mother-and-daughter shopping trips.

What a coward I've become! Maeve thought. Even though she trembled inside at the notion of going out in public, the possibility of a grandchild brought home as nothing else had just how limited her existence had become. That was no legacy to pass along to the next generation.

She squared her shoulders and nodded. "I would." But she clutched Harry's neck as she did so. As before, the feel of him comforted.

"I know it'll be hard, but it'd mean the world to me," Penny said, doing some clutching of her own on Maeve's arm. Then she shook her head. "We can't get ahead of ourselves. They warned us to prepare for disappointment. Some teenage mothers change their minds at the last minute." She was visibly steeling herself against this new possibility for pain.

Maeve cupped her daughter's cheeks with her hands. "We'll get through it. You have a truly fine man at your side, and you know your brothers and I will be there for you, whatever happens." She pasted on a reassuring smile she didn't quite feel. "The first thing I'm going to do is not wimp out on the shelter."

"I wondered if you would talk to me about it. Gerty said something happened to you there yesterday. What was it?"

"A man, Charles Lawrence. He was there and recognized me."

"The oilman? Craig has mentioned him, I think. At any rate, we've seen him at several functions around town. I think he dates Cecily Dunstan."

Maeve hadn't considered that she could ask Craig about him, but her son-in-law was a banker with many ties in the business community, and he was someone she trusted implicitly. "I'd like to get Craig's opinion of him."

"Why? What did he say to you?"

"Very little. I didn't give him a chance." *I ran. Like a scared rabbit.* She cast her gaze down. "He said he meant me no harm, but…"

Penny grimaced. "That was your one refuge. Were you thinking you wouldn't go back?"

"I was," Maeve admitted. "I just…" She lifted her hands. "I only want to be normal. To live my life and be left alone."

"I could kill Alyssa Ritchie." Penny rose and began to pace.

But Alyssa Ritchie wasn't the major source of Penny's pain. Penny had been her daddy's girl, and his desertion was a terrible blow before they'd ever heard of the Ritchie woman. Far beyond the financial crisis he'd precipitated, Hilton had wounded his daughter deeply by proving to be someone very different from the man Penny had adored. In addition, because Penny had kept much of her money invested in his bank stock despite Craig's pleas to her to divest it, she was yet another investor who'd lost much of the savings she'd accumulated from her modeling career.

"Have you been to see him in jail?" Maeve asked.

Penny shook her head. "I don't want to. You?"

"No." Craig had pressed Maeve to file for divorce early in the crisis to separate herself from any liability for Hilton's actions. The divorce proceedings were under way, but a part of her wanted to ask Hilton, just once, why he'd betrayed her, betrayed their whole family, in so many ways. A larger part, though, wanted never to lay eyes on the man again.

But he was Penny's father, and she had to come to some sort of peace with herself. Maeve wished she knew what that might be.

Their earlier happiness was threatened by thoughts of Hilton, and Maeve couldn't bear for him to do any more damage to them. She searched for a lighter topic, and her gaze lit on Harry. Then she looked at Penny again. "So would you like to take a walk with Harry and me? Can you stay for dinner? Is Craig free?"

Penny's expression was grateful. She glanced down at the dog and smiled. "I would love to. I can't wait for Craig to meet Daddy's replacement."

"Penelope!" Maeve burst out laughing.

When her daughter joined her, Maeve uttered a silent thanksgiving. *We will make it. My family will get through this.*

Even if I'm not exactly sure how.

"MAEVE DOESN'T WANT to talk to you," said the same woman who had answered once before at the Branch residence, but she'd hung up on Chuck as soon as he'd given his name.

"I want to hear that from her."

"I'll call the police if you don't leave us alone." A pause. "How did you get this number, anyway? We had it changed."

Chuck dodged the question. Money had its uses, but his answer was unlikely to endear him to Maeve's gatekeeper. He wasn't exactly sure why he was trying again. He was a busy man. If the woman didn't want his help, he should walk away.

But he couldn't. Not until he'd spoken to Maeve Branch directly. Taken her measure. His own mother had been left high and dry when he was a boy. Her struggles still touched him, and she hadn't had to bear the added burden of scandal.

"I mean her no harm, I swear. That day at the shelter, she seemed so...bruised."

"Bruised isn't the half of it," the woman muttered. "That *schweine* has nearly killed her. And his tramp isn't helping."

"Alyssa Ritchie is a piece of work, all right. As is Maeve's husband."

"Not husband for long. The divorce can't come too soon." The woman uttered a low growl of disgust. "For all the good it will do Maeve."

"She's in a lot of trouble, isn't she?" He waited through the long silence. "I'm sorry. That's private."

"No one else honors her privacy, so why should you? The vultures in the press, the so-called friends who only want to gather gossip... She has no one to trust but her children and me."

"She's lucky to have you on her side."

"Humph." Clearly this woman had Maeve's back and would not be easily persuaded.

But he hadn't made his fortune by giving up at the first sign of resistance. "Hilton Branch once asked me to joint-venture with him on a project," he said. "I refused. He didn't mind cutting corners, and his ethics troubled me."

Another long silence. "Well, you have some sense, at least," she said grudgingly at last.

"That's where I met Maeve, at that dinner in her home. She was the perfect hostess."

"That's her, all right."

He ventured further. "But she was very quiet. I took it for being remote, for being cold, but I'm wondering if I might have misjudged her."

"You wouldn't be the first."

He suspected that was right. Maeve had a reputation for being an ice queen, but the woman he'd seen at the shelter was nothing like that. "Is she shy?"

"Always has been. A real homebody, but still she

did everything that horrible man asked of her." Then the woman seemed to recover herself. "This is Maeve's business, not yours."

"I agree, except for one thing."

"And what might that be?"

"First, would you tell me your name, Maeve's protector?" In a good negotiation, there had to be reciprocation.

"Why?"

"Because I like to know who I'm dealing with."

"You won't be doing anything but hanging up. We have nothing to discuss. Maeve doesn't want to talk to you."

"I wonder."

"What does that mean?"

"Does she even know I've called?"

This silence was the longest yet.

"I thought so," he said. "You care about her, that much is obvious."

"Of course I do."

"Then aren't you at least a little curious about why I didn't give up the first time?"

"No," she said too quickly.

"I think you are. Can you afford to turn away help for her?"

He could almost hear her brain clicking. "Tell me why you'd want to help."

"Tell me your name, and I will."

Her dilemma was nearly audible through the phone.

Finally she spoke. "Don't know why it matters, but don't see the harm. I'm Gertrude Hoffman. I was her housekeeper for many years."

"But not now?"

"You got my name. Now explain yourself."

He stifled a chuckle at her tenacity. "My father left my mother stranded with me when I was six years old. We had nothing. I watched her struggle to make ends meet, and I tried to help, but I couldn't do for her what she needed most. I couldn't heal her broken heart and I couldn't make the money we desperately needed."

"You were only a child."

"That didn't stop me from worrying about her and feeling useless." He paused, surprised to find remnants of that boy's shame still within him. He frowned and continued. "When I was eight, I took on a paper route, and I've worked ever since. I bought my mother a decent house as soon as I could, and I tried to make up for what she'd been through, but she died in her forties, so she never had the chance to benefit from the wealth I've accumulated. And she never got over my father's desertion."

"You did all you could, Mr. Lawrence."

"Chuck. Call me Chuck."

"We'll see." The jury was still out, apparently.

"So I never gave Maeve's situation much thought when the scandal broke, Gertrude. I'm sorry to say that. Of course, it was in all the papers and on TV, but I assumed she had money of her own and plenty of friends and all. That day at the shelter, however, the woman I saw…it took me a while to recognize her, and what I saw was not the woman I thought she was."

"Because she looks terrible?"

"No. Because she looks broken." He was surprised at himself. Something about Maeve had reached out to him, even while she was running away.

"She's been through a lot. She loves animals, and being there heals something in her." A pause. "It's just about the only time she goes out in public."

Damn. "And I scared her off."

"You did. I'm afraid she won't go back to the shelter now. Did you tell anyone who she really is?"

"No."

"Well, that's something, anyway."

"Will you tell her I called?"

In the ensuing pause, he could hear Gertrude's breathing. "Why?"

"I want to help her."

"How?"

"I really can't know that until I understand her situation better. For that, I have to talk to her."

A deep sigh. "I'll give her the message, Mr. Lawrence. But you better not be messing with her."

"I'm not, I promise. Thank you, Gertrude."

Another harrumph. "Give me your phone number, Mr. Lawrence."

"Chuck." He told her his home, cell and business numbers. "Goodbye, Gertrude."

"Goodbye, Mr. Lawrence."

He was grinning when he hung up the phone.

Two DAYS LATER, Maeve still hadn't called. He didn't have time for this distraction, but he wasn't a man to simply give up and wash his hands of her just because she was a lot of trouble—though God knows maybe he should. If only that image of her, the vulnerable woman in jeans and no makeup, would quit popping into his head.

He glanced at his calendar and realized that tomorrow would be one week since he'd seen her at the shelter.

Perhaps he needed to schedule a follow-up visit. He had all the information he needed and had, in fact, asked his architect to sketch out some preliminary proposals for the wing he wanted to donate. There was no real reason for him to go.

Except that a certain woman might be there.

His very participation in a much-needed expansion meant that the shelter would welcome him any time he wished to drop by. He didn't make it a practice to take advantage of his status as benefactor.

But perhaps he would, very soon.

Like tomorrow.

CHAPTER FOUR

MAEVE STOOD at her kitchen sink, staring out as Harry sniffed his way around the backyard. She'd lived in this house ever since her wedding day, and so many memories were bound up in it, not all of them bad.

She glanced over at the latest self-help book she'd tried in her effort to begin to understand what she should have understood long ago. That any grown woman would let herself be snookered into giving up control of her life the way she had with Hilton was beyond shameful.

That she'd done it willingly was far worse.

And now she might lose everything because of it. Her father was surely rolling over in his grave—though he, too, had welcomed Hilton into the family with open arms.

She bowed her head for a second and, once again, considered not returning to the shelter today, however much it had been such a rare source of pleasure during dark times. She wasn't afraid of encountering that man again, she told herself. That wasn't it.

There was so much else she needed to be doing—learning how to pick her way through the minefield of her finances, first and foremost. The firm that had once been so eager to act as her financial adviser had lost interest once the full extent of Hilton's perfidy had become clear. Last week, when she'd placed an urgent phone call to the firm and still had not received an answer, she'd realized that she was on her own. With all the criminal charges that had been filed, never mind all the civil suits that were bound to come, nearly everything she and Hilton owned was in jeopardy.

She'd clung to the hope that Hilton would return or be found with the embezzled funds intact, that somehow things could be set aright. When Hilton had been charged and extradited, that hope had faded. Much of the embezzled funds had gone to support his lifestyle, including the mistress of twenty years. The web of his deceit was only now being untangled, but it didn't look promising—a snarl of excess and high-risk investments that hadn't paid off.

The divorce Craig had insisted Maeve file early on wasn't yet final, but its purpose had been to protect her remaining assets. The modest trust fund from her father wasn't nearly enough to support the upkeep on this huge house or pay the property taxes, much less provide for her future.

So the adviser, seeing nothing to gain, had taken a powder, and Maeve was on her own. She hadn't yet told her children about the defection of those they believed would help her, and she didn't want to. A banker himself, Craig offered advice, but he was busy with his new job and upcoming fatherhood. Maeve was not a doddering old woman who needed to be taken care of.

But oh, sweet heaven, how little she understood about how to care for herself when it came to money. She'd never finished college and had no job skills, even if she wasn't beyond the age most employers would welcome.

The piper would have to be paid soon, and she was terrified of the reckoning.

Which was why she slept little, poring over the papers Hilton had left behind, trying to make sense of unfamiliar terminology. She'd forced herself to learn how to use the computer, which she'd hardly touched before Hilton had defected, grateful for the wonderful how-to books for "dummies."

Which she surely was, letting herself get into this pickle. How had she rationalized what now seemed like criminal ignorance, a willing blindness not only to the details of finances she'd never cared to delve into but to the basic nature of the man with whom she'd brought four children into the world?

She'd been raised by a very traditional couple who divided their duties along gender lines, true— but hadn't she come to adulthood during the women's movement? She'd buried her head in the sand of diapers and play groups, of homemaking— if doing so with household help could be called such—and focused on feathering her nest.

So now she was paying.

She glanced over at the stack of files she'd been trying to decipher last night, stocks that had been bought and sold, with words like "capital gains" and "share cost-averaging" that made her eyes blur.

She shouldn't go to the shelter; she should stay right here and try again.

Then she heard Gerty's car pull up outside and she snatched the stack of files, hustling them back to the locked filing cabinet. She trusted Gerty with her life, but she couldn't ask her friend to share this burden. Her kids, either.

This cross was her own to bear.

The phone rang just as she was locking the file drawer. "Hello?"

"Hey, Mom."

"Will." She smiled with sincere pleasure. "How are you, sweetie? Are you in Kansas yet? Have I told you lately how proud I am of you for making the Chase this year?" She was referring to the Chase for the NASCAR Sprint Cup.

"I'm next to last in the points, Mom. I fell five spots the first race."

Her eldest twin was possessed of his father's mercurial personality and drive, and that often cost him. His temper often trumped his judgment, unlike his more controlled twin, Bart.

That didn't mean she loved him any less. "You didn't cause that crash, Will. It's still early. You're not out of contention by any means."

"It's a lot of pressure. My cars haven't been running all that great lately, and we can't seem to get them dialed in. Another race or two of trouble, and I'm out of luck altogether."

"You've always done well on intermediate tracks, though."

"You're amazing, Mom," he said.

"Why?"

"I bet not one of the women at your country club knows jack about NASCAR, much less understands the points or recognizes the difference in tracks. Did you ever imagine, when you were a little girl, that you would?"

She had to grin at that. "Your grandfather would have sent me to the convent for hanging around a track."

Will laughed. "Have I thanked you lately for being such a great mom?"

Unbearably touched, it was a moment before she could answer. "Thank you, sweetheart. That means the world to me."

"So enough of my woes. How are you doing?"

"I'm fine."

"You always say that. I have to call Gerty or Penny to get the scoop."

"I'm surrounded by spies, am I?" She knew very well that her children and Gerty talked about her, and Lord knows she'd given them reason.

"They just love you. We all do. What Hilton did—" His voice hardened.

Maeve grieved that the twins refused to call their father Dad as they once had, since Hilton's misdeeds had come to light. They'd foregone their chance to visit him in jail in Charlotte right after his arrest, and both had hardened their hearts against him. Not that she blamed them, exactly. Hilton had put both boys' racing careers in jeopardy, in addition to everything else. Hilton didn't deserve them, but she mourned their loss of a father figure. Hilton had been a flawed one, but he'd been so proud of his twins.

"Honey, I'm so glad you've found a new sponsor. I don't guess we'll ever understand why your father lied to us all, but we have to move on."

"You're not saying you can forgive him, are you, Mom? He hurt you worse than any of us. I could kill him for what he did to you."

"Sweetheart, you don't mean that."

"I do. I hate the bastard. He's dead to me, but that's not really enough—"

"Will, don't." Maeve could hear his temper rising, and that was the last thing he needed now. He had to focus on his career and block out everything else. "Please don't do this to yourself. You have a lot on the line now, and that's where your energies need to be directed. You concentrate on your driving. There are only eight races left, and I want you to come to the end of this season and be proud of yourself for giving it your best shot, as proud as I am. You've done something remarkable, you and Bart both, to be in the Chase in only your second year. Don't let your father take that victory from you. You've battled past all the distractions this year, and you deserve a happy ending."

"Only one of your boys can win, Mom."

She sighed even as she smiled ruefully. "I know. It would have been so much easier if only one of you liked to race."

There was a smile in his voice, too. "We'll always be competitors, Bart and me."

"As long as you don't stop being best friends and brothers."

"Not a chance. We fight—we always have—but I know Bart's got my back, and I have his. Except at the finish line, of course."

Having twins, both so fiercely competitive, had always been complicated, but even if she could she wouldn't change a thing.

"Bart's in sixth going into this race, Mom. Means you have to root for me this time."

Maeve chuckled. Neither of them had ever understood how she could cheer for both every time. They'd decided between themselves that she was allowed to root for the underdog whenever they competed, understanding her emotional makeup. God help her when they were tied—thank heaven it didn't happen often. "You've got it." She crossed her fingers, though, knowing she would always be cheering for them both.

"Mom…?" Will paused, and she wondered what he was hesitant to say.

"What is it?"

"Do you…" He halted. "Do you think you'll ever come back to the track?"

"Oh, honey…" He might be thirty years old, but he was still her child, and she was freshly aware of how much she'd let all her children down by hiding from the glare of publicity. "I am so sorry. I want to, but—"

"It's okay, Mom." But she could hear his disappointment.

Everything in her quailed at the very notion of confronting the world where Hilton had been so well-known, if not universally liked.

But this was her son asking. His brother probably felt the same, and through all the years of their growing up, she'd never missed a soccer game, a school program or a single race, not until Hilton had smashed her cocoon into bits.

It was time. Past time. She clenched the fingers of her free hand tightly and steeled herself. "I can't make it this week, honey." *I can't afford the airfare, for one thing.* And she would not ask him to help. "But count on me at Talladega." She would get there somehow.

"Really?" Will sounded about six years old, both thrilled and fearful of disappointment.

"Really."

"Mom, that's awesome. Are you sure you're okay with it?"

No. "Absolutely," she replied. "I watch every week on television, but it's not the same."

"Oh, man. Bart will go nuts. This is great, Mom. Really great."

For the excitement in his voice, she would scale mountains.

She was terrified.

No. She was a mother, and that was what a good mother did, supported her children in whatever they attempted. Her boys had been facing the public scrutiny all this time, and the least she could do was be by their sides.

"You can sit in Jim Latimer's or Gideon Taney's suite, you know that. I'll even ask Taney if he can send the plane for you, and I'll get back to you with the details. You can stay in my motor home or Bart's, whichever you prefer. I'll get you a hard card to allow you full access, so you'll be good to go."

"You don't have to do all that, darling."

"Mom," he said, "I'd walk to Texas and carry you on my shoulders if that's what it would take." Then he grew serious. "But be honest. How much do you dread this? What can I do to make it easier on you?" He paused. "You don't have to go, not if it's going to be too hard."

A rush of love swamped her, that he would still give up what he wanted so much, for her sake. "Branches don't quit," she said.

"MacGregors," he replied. "I'm not sure I want to be a Branch anymore. If it wouldn't create such a mess, I'd change my name."

The wounds Hilton had inflicted went so deep.

For that alone, the hurt he'd dealt their children, she could never forgive Hilton. "Oh, honey. Don't spare him another thought." *He's not all bad,* she wanted to be able to say, but right now, she couldn't think of one virtue Hilton possessed.

She forced herself to brighten. "You just get ready for Kansas and know I'm cheering for you every lap."

"But not Bart, right?" The teasing note so characteristic of him—and too long missing—was back.

She laughed. "Well, while I'm talking to you, at least," she teased in response.

"Man, Mom—" his voice thickened "—it is so great to hear you laugh. I've missed that."

Guilt rolled over her at how she'd failed her children. Yes, they were grown, but they still needed to know they could count on her. Sawyer had been in trouble and not told her. Penny had nearly sacrificed her marriage. The twins were engaged in a challenging sport but had fought to keep going even while the world they'd known had fallen apart.

In that moment, she resolved to refocus on her family. The rest of her battles she'd fight one step at a time.

Somehow—she had no idea how—she would find her way out of this morass. Get back to being her children's mother. It was the only thing she'd ever been good at.

"I'm sorry, sweetheart. I've let you down, but I won't be doing that any longer."

"Don't you dare be rough on yourself, Mom. That bastard did a number on you, and you got slammed. But you just remember that we're not babies anymore, none of us."

She could barely speak as tears rolled down her cheeks. "I love you, Will, so much." She grasped for a tissue.

"I love you, too, Mom. We all do." A pause. "You can change your mind about Talladega if you're not ready."

But she heard the hope in his voice. "No. I've hidden long enough. I will be there, I promise."

"Thanks, Mom. That's awesome. Can't wait to tell my baby brother." The light tone let her know he didn't mean Sawyer, her youngest, but Bart, younger than Will by two minutes. Nothing riled Bart more than Will calling him baby brother.

"Troublemaker," she said. "Go get 'em, tiger. Kansas hasn't seen the like of the Branch boys."

"Love you, Mom."

"Love you, too, sweetheart. Give your brother a kiss for me."

"Yeah, that's gonna happen. You'll have to settle for a manly slug on the arm."

But if she knew her boys, there would be at least one back-slapping hug involved. "Okay. Wimp."

Will was laughing as he disconnected.

And Maeve found herself smiling past her tears.

CHAPTER FIVE

CHUCK WAS RELIEVED to see Maeve's car parked in the shelter lot when he arrived. *Margaret,* he corrected himself. *Don't out her to the staff.* Her identity was hers to keep.

He strode into the office. Carolyn Mason jumped to her feet, the line between her brows conveying her anxiety. "Mr. Lawrence? Something I can do for you? Er, do you have more questions or—"

He should have thought about the panic he could create. "No, no, you did an excellent job the other day, Carolyn. I just…" He cast about for a good reason to be here. "I've seen some preliminary sketches from the architect, and I thought I might get a better sense of them if I were on-site."

"Oh!" Her whole face brightened. "Sketches? Do you have them?"

"I'm sorry, I don't. I believe that the architect wanted to consult with you before proceeding." He resorted to a smile. "I simply like being hands-on with my donations."

That was not strictly true. He could have bitten his

tongue when he saw her frown forming. Holding the purse strings could make some philanthropists into tyrants, but Chuck had never been one of them. It was his personal policy to be certain of the worth of the cause, then to let those with day-to-day understanding decide what to do with the funds. If they weren't to be trusted, he shouldn't be contributing to them.

"It's all right, Carolyn," he said. "I promise I won't encroach. I'd like to look around a little, then be out of your hair."

"Sure," she hastened to say. "If you can just give me a second…"

He saw the stack of paperwork on her battered desk and seized on the excuse. "I remember my way around. If you'll trust me…?"

"Oh." Her face lit. "Yes, absolutely." Then her expression dimmed again. "But there are animals who could hurt you, Mr. Lawrence."

He held up one hand in a Scout promise. "I swear I won't stick my hand into cages. Or the animals' mouths."

"That would be good," she said.

He forced back a smile at her seriousness. "All right, then. I won't be long." *Just long enough to find the ice queen in disguise.*

"Take your time. Let someone know if you need anything."

Even better. *Maeve, come with me. Your manager said so.* Chuck amused himself with the possibilities for what Maeve would say back to him. Did she ever curse?

Then he sobered. She wasn't an ice queen, he was all but certain now. And she didn't need anyone giving her a hard time, even in jest. He opened the door that led to the kennels, the din increasingly loud. Small yaps, big barks and some piteous whining.

And that was just the dogs. The cats, stacked in cage on top of cage, made their own ruckus.

He didn't know how Maeve stood it. He loved dogs as much as the next man, but this was miserable. He was glad he could help make it better, but she'd been dealing with this for years, apparently. How did she continue?

He escaped the first wing and headed outside, the tension in his shoulders easing as the volume decreased.

"You're here," said a voice behind him. "Gerty warned me."

He whirled to see Maeve with a mutt of overpowering ugliness. She was scratching it behind the ears. "Warned you? I thought she'd decided she liked me."

She didn't mirror his grin. "What do you want from me?"

This woman wasn't broken, not the way she'd been last week. He wondered what had happened, even as he applauded the change. He'd disliked seeing her look so beaten. If a little stronger, however, she was still wary.

"I don't want anything from you but a chance."

She frowned. "To do what? Entertain your golf partner or spice up the next charity ball with stories of poor Maeve?"

"Ever get tired of lugging around that chip on your shoulder?"

"What?" She looked as shocked as he felt. He hadn't meant to unload on her, but damn it, she shouldn't question his ethics.

"First, I don't play golf. Waste of time. Second, all I want is to help you."

"I don't need your help."

"Is that right. What will you do when property taxes on that white elephant are due at the end of the year? What happens when spring comes, and you can't afford to pay a gardener? You plan to take care of that house and grounds all by yourself, or are you thinking Gertrude will come out of retirement?"

She literally backed up a step. "You…" She drew herself straight. Fire sparked in her eyes. "You have no right to invade my privacy."

"Everyone else seems to want to, and they'll continue until you get your act together."

"How dare you!" She wheeled away from him. "This conversation is over."

He caught up to her. Stepped in front and held up his hands. "Look, I'm not the enemy. I can help you. You don't know how you're going to fix your financial problems, do you?"

"Get out of my way."

"No." When her gaze whipped up to his, he grinned. "Doesn't it feel better to be mad than beaten down?"

"What?" Her eyes narrowed. "Are you saying you made me angry on purpose?"

"No," he replied. "It was only a side benefit."

She tried to swerve around him, but he blocked her neatly. "Look, give me this one chance. Meet me for coffee after you finish here today."

"Why?" She seemed sincerely curious. "Why do you care what happens to me?"

"I'll explain." He arched one brow. "If you'll meet me."

"I don't want to."

"But you have to come out of hiding sometime."

Her eyes sparked again, and he waited for the retort.

Instead, she smiled ruefully. "You're right about that."

"So you'll let me buy you a coffee? Or dinner?"

Dinner was apparently the wrong word to use, he could tell instantly. Sounded too much like a date, maybe. To his surprise, the idea had appeal.

Of course, he wasn't really clear on exactly why it did. "Only to talk," he amended. "You have to eat, right?" He glanced over her slender figure. "Though it doesn't look like you've been doing much of that." The woman he recalled had been rounder. Now she was approaching gaunt.

"My diet is none of your business." She studied him. "All right. But only coffee. And I'll meet you."

"What time do you leave here?"

"Three."

"Let's do Café Matisse at three-fifteen. It's nearby."

"I know where it is."

"Good."

He lingered, at a loss now that he'd gotten his way. "So…want to show me around now?"

Her expression chided him. "Mr. Lawrence, you've had the tour already."

"Chuck. And I might have missed something."

"No, Chuck," she said, inflecting his name with meaning he couldn't quite decipher. "I don't believe you missed anything. Goodbye." She turned to go.

He stood watching her for several seconds. Wondered if she'd really show up later.

Then he grinned. He'd be back here at two-thirty, just in case. His crowded schedule would require some rearranging, but for some reason, he didn't mind as much as he should have.

He left, shaking his head. This Galahad stuff was a lot of work.

NEARLY SIX HOURS later, Maeve glanced down at her filthy clothes. She'd bathed one too many animals, and she not only looked as if she'd rolled around with them in the dirt, but she smelled unmistakably of dog.

If only she had a change of clothes with her. Why had she agreed to meet him so soon after her shift?

Why had she agreed to meet him at all?

The man could give lessons in persistence, and she could not, for the life of her, figure out why he was so intent on her. It wasn't like she was any prize to look at—she had foregone the surgeries many in her set considered de rigueur—so while she'd taken care to protect her skin to offset the time she spent in her garden, she had wrinkles and looked her age. She had sags where she once had not. And she'd never been a beauty, anyway. Passably pretty was all she could claim, but lately, the sleepless nights and, drat him for noticing, the skipped meals, had taken their toll. Once she'd have jumped through hoops to be this thin— hadn't she tried several diets with little result?—but she'd discovered the most effective one by accident.

The Desertion, Destitution and Divorce Diet. Maeve had to grin. Maybe she should get it copyrighted. Not that she'd wish the past several months on her worst enemy.

She couldn't do this. Could not meet this man, and it wasn't about her appearance. Well, not totally. She hardly knew him from Adam, and she could see no good reason he should spare her even a second to help when he no doubt had a full load of responsibilities without her.

But he'd seemed sincerely affronted when she'd accused him of wishing simply to gather juicy gossip. Something about him seemed trustworthy, but who was she to credit her instincts? Yes, she'd known Hilton was full of himself and deeply ambitious, but she'd never once dreamed he'd desert her and their children or leave them in such straits, much less that he'd carried on with some bimbo for twenty years.

Twenty years! Bought her a condo, taken her with him on a legion of business trips... How could she not have suspected?

Maeve stared in the mirror of the tiny bathroom at the shelter and wondered how she would ever trust her judgment again.

Or why she would want to gamble on meeting this man, this big, rugged, handsome tycoon who probably had women at his beck and call. What on earth could he want from her?

And how could she go, looking so awful? Café Matisse, of all places, where it would be all too easy to run into some of her so-called friends.

She couldn't. She wouldn't. She glanced at her watch and saw that she had twelve minutes remaining on her shift. Still not enough, even with the fifteen more minutes before their meeting, to race home and change.

How shallow to care about her appearance when her whole existence was in jeopardy. She was ashamed and embarrassed and absolutely certain that she had no choice but to head straight home and never see the man again.

Except that he knew where to find her, and she didn't want to give up this respite, at least not until the inevitable time that she had to find a job, doing

God knows what, to support herself. She was fiddling while Rome burned, she knew, and she couldn't keep doing it much longer.

She spoke to one of the techs as she left through the back. "Tell Carolyn I have to go just a little early, and I'm sorry." Though she didn't have to be; she was a volunteer, and the shelter staff was grateful for whatever they got. Maeve, however, prided herself on being reliable. She'd missed less than a handful of shifts in the five years she'd been coming here, and never for frivolous reasons.

"Sure thing," the man said.

Maeve hurried to her car, resolving to find out if Gerty had Lawrence's phone number so she could at least be polite enough to call and tell him she wouldn't be meeting him, after all—

"Yep, thought so. Sneaking out, are you?"

Her head whipped up at the sound of his voice. Chuck Lawrence was leaning leisurely against the trunk of her car, his posture conveying the lazy certainty of a big cat who knows his quarry is neatly trapped.

"I was—"

"Not going to meet me, right?" There was a gleam in his eye, an amusement that really got her dander up.

"I was going to call you and cancel," she said stiffly.

"Ah, yes…the perfect lady and her excellent manners. And what would you have given as your reason?"

"I don't owe you a reason. I don't owe you anything." She brushed ineffectually at the drying mud on her shirt.

"Oh," he said. "I'm sorry. I didn't think."

"Think what?"

He nodded at her clothes. "Café Matisse is a hotbed of the do-nothing wives. I should have considered that you wouldn't feel comfortable there."

"Or maybe *you* wouldn't. Wouldn't serve your reputation, now would it?"

He cocked his head. "What reputation?"

She flicked a hand. "Men like you, with a different young babe on your arm every week, with too much money and time on your hands."

He glared at her for a second, then surprised her by throwing his head back and laughing. She stood there, rigid, then decided he'd surely move if she started backing her car out. She'd taken one step when he grabbed her arm.

"I loved my wife. I would have given anything to have her until we were both very old, but I wasn't given that choice, nor was she." All humor had fled.

Suddenly Maeve recalled that he was a widower, not a divorced man. "I'm sorry. That was wrong of me."

"One other thing—I made my money by the sweat of my brow. I busted my ass for years as a roughneck. Nobody gave me a dime or a helping hand while I built my fortune. I'm a regular guy. I didn't date at all for four years after she died, and I wouldn't date a young babe if you paid me." He let go. "I wanted to help you because my mother was once in your shoes, and she had no one. But I'm done offering. You have to trust someone sometime, not that I can't imagine how hard that is right now." He leaned closer, looming over her. "But get this straight, Miss Silver Spoon. You don't know me. I'm not a *type*." He stepped back and turned, then paused. "Gertrude has my phone numbers, if you change your mind."

He started to walk away. Maeve was suffused with shame at her behavior. She'd never been one to cast judgment on people, and it wasn't like her to go on the attack or be so ungrateful. Trusting anyone was hard for her now, but she didn't much like the person she was turning into.

"Wait!" she called.

His pace slowed, but he didn't stop.

"Please," she said. "I'm sorry. I just…"

He faced her but didn't speak.

"I…you're right. I don't know who to believe anymore, and I'm scared half to death." She pressed her lips together before continuing. "But I don't like being scared. I have to figure all this out, and I don't know how." It was a bitter admission.

She glanced at her attire. "I'd rather not go to Café Matisse looking like this. I wish I didn't care, but I do."

"Where would you feel comfortable going?"

Relief rushed through her that he seemed to be giving her another chance. "I don't really know. And

I'm very sorry about your mother, but I don't want your pity." She smiled wryly. "I think I might have been pitying myself enough without anyone else contributing."

"There's an old-style coffee shop out on Abrams Road. No one you know would ever be there. They make great bad-for-you breakfasts the old way. Its customers cross the spectrum but mostly contractors and such, so no one would bat an eye at what's on your clothes."

She nodded and tried to smile at his thoughtfulness. "Where on Abrams?"

"I could…" *Take you,* he'd probably meant to say, but he didn't finish. "East of the Tollway. I'll drive slowly so you can follow."

She swallowed hard. "Thank you. I'm honestly sorry about what I said."

"Forget it," he replied, then turned. "See you there." With his long legs, he quickly strode out of sight.

Chastened, Maeve got into her car and wondered if he'd really wait for her. How much she'd insulted him.

But when she got to the street, he was parked just past the entrance. He waved and started moving.

Nervous, grateful, afraid to hope that he could really help, not at all sure what she wanted from this man and definitely not certain what he wanted from her, Maeve tried to focus only on keeping his car in sight.

CHAPTER SIX

HE WASN'T WRONG. This place was an old-fashioned diner, with counter seating, as well as cracked-vinyl booths. The air was a thick soup of bacon and onions, French fries, grilled burgers and coffee—the old kind, straight up. Not a latte in sight.

Mr. Lawrence—Chuck, she corrected herself—escorted her to a booth near the back. She slid inside and noted, with amusement, the jukebox at each booth. There was a place in trendy Deep Ellum with jukeboxes, but it was run by kids looking for a gimmick. These ones were old and grimy, and as she glanced through the selections, definitely original to the place. "My word," she said. "I haven't heard these songs in years. 'Blueberry Hill' by Fats Domino, old Johnny Cash, Hank Williams…"

"Not exactly your style, is it?"

Her eyes narrowed. "Mr. Lawrence, you say I don't know you."

"Chuck."

She clasped her fingers together, then forced

herself to nod. "Did it ever occur to you, *Chuck,* that you might not know me, either?"

He grinned, unrepentant. "I really like it when you get all prim on me."

She could practically feel flames shooting from her ears. "I am not prim."

"You are, actually. It seems to be your protective shield. Princess to peasant works with most people. Keeps them at a distance."

She wasn't sure how she felt about him seeing into her like that. "But not you, apparently."

His head dipped in salute. "There you go." As if she were a bright pupil.

"Have you always been so full of yourself, Mr.—" At his arched eyebrow, she amended, "Chuck?"

"I'd still be in Odessa if I wasn't. Only I'd be a broken-down former roughneck living in a trailer, collecting Social Security."

"I don't believe you're old enough for Social Security."

"Busted. No, I'm fifty-seven, but the rest of it's accurate."

"A self-made man?"

"Pretty much."

"And clever, too, I imagine."

"And if we keep talking about me, we'll never have to talk about you."

She studied him, uncertain how to respond. How much to reveal.

The waitress saved her by approaching. "What'll you folks have?"

"Coffee for two and a hamburger for the lady."

Maeve frowned. "It's the middle of the afternoon."

"But you didn't have lunch, did you? And you haven't been eating." He nodded at the waitress. "Bring me one, too, so she'll have company. Make mine medium rare. What about you?" He was looking at Maeve now.

She was torn between indignation at his presumption and a lovely sense of being cared for. But he was right—she did need to eat. If she waited until she got home, she'd wind up having soup or cereal. Or nothing. "Medium," she huffed. Then jutted her chin at him. "With onions. Lots of them."

A slow grin crossed his lips, and the woman in Maeve couldn't help responding, however much doing so shocked her.

Good grief. The last thing she needed was a man in her life.

The waitress left, returning quickly with coffee. Silence hovered between Maeve and Chuck.

When she left again, his eyes locked on Maeve. "How much do you understand about your finances?"

She blinked. "You have more gall than anyone I've ever met. That's none of your business."

"I've done my research. You've led a sheltered life. And you're kidding yourself if you think that Hilton's finances will remain secret now that he's been arrested and charged. Everything about your life is going to become public property."

She gripped her hands tightly around the coffee cup. "I feel like everything is already."

"I only want to help, Maeve. What you say goes no further." He paused, then tried again. "I had the sense from Hilton in our brief acquaintance that he made the financial decisions. And I'm sorry, but from what's come out thus far, it appears there's a lot you didn't know."

She kept her eyes on the circle of brown liquid, afraid she would cry. Or shatter. Finally, she nodded.

"Do you have advisers you trust?" he asked gently.

She shook her head. Spoke softly. "I thought I did, but once Hilton was…arrested—" she cleared her throat "—and confessed that most of the money was gone so there'd be no big fee for them, they quit returning my calls." She lifted her head then. "I do not want my children to know this. Bart found this firm for me, and he would worry." She took a deep breath and continued. "I've been trying to read up, and I found some files, but—" she spread her hands "—it's so much to learn, so much that's confusing. I don't have a lot of time."

"I have people who can handle this for you."

"I can't afford them." Admitting it galled her.

"They won't charge you."

Her head whipped up. "No. I don't want charity." However much she might need it. Not yet, and please, God, not ever.

"All right." He nodded at her. "I respect that. I think you're going to have to accept help at some point, though." He ignored her shaking head. "For now, however, what about this? Why don't you ask me some questions about what has confused you, and I'll see if I'm any good at explaining the concepts."

His tone was pure kindness, and she should be grateful. She was, but it was all so embarrassing. "It's pathetic. *I'm* pathetic." Suddenly, all the shame she'd kept private somehow rushed to the surface. "How can a grown woman be so blind? So stupid?" Her throat was tight with unshed tears. She looked out the window, struggling for control.

"You are anything but stupid, Maeve. Blind, maybe, perhaps even willfully so, but you can change that if you're willing to work at it." His voice was matter-of-fact and not judgmental.

The very evenness of his response helped her regain her composure. She looked him straight in the eye. "I am not lazy. I never have been."

"Good. Then let's get to work. Ask me a question."

She began with purely theoretical ones, the meaning of terms such as "capital gains," how mutual funds worked, what were risky investments and what types were safer. She wasn't ready to admit to anyone yet how bleak her future seemed, so the questions that haunted her—*Will I lose my home? How on earth will I find a job? Where will I live?*

How will I live?—would remain her private nightmares for now.

Their food arrived, and she tucked into her meal like a starving wolf, surprised at how hungry she was. "This is amazing." She glanced up to see him staring at her with something that approached fondness. "What?"

"I like to see a woman enjoy her food. So few do anymore, too caught up in being ultra-thin, picking their way through a meal that looks like rabbit food."

"I don't normally eat like a trucker, but—" she shrugged "—I'm also not usually this thin, more's the pity."

"Real women have hips, however little you all seem to believe that anymore."

"Oh, I have hips, all right."

"I remember that. From that night, at your home."

She blushed and set her hamburger down. Frowned. "You shouldn't be noticing."

"Sue me. I'm not blind."

She couldn't figure out what to think of him. No man had ever spoken so frankly to her, except her husband. But his words hadn't been compliments. "Hilton always wanted me to lose weight."

"Hilton was an asshole. I thought you were stunning. Icy, maybe, but a looker nonetheless."

Maeve could barely keep her jaw from dropping. Stunning? A looker? "You did not."

"Suit yourself. I know what I saw."

Then she recalled the other part. "Icy? I am not—"

"I get that now. You're reserved, maybe even shy, aren't you? But you have to agree that Hilton's an asshole."

He grinned, and she couldn't help smiling back. "I've never used that word, but—"

He waved off her permission. "Maybe you should."

She bit her lip, then said, nearly under her breath, "Hilton's an asshole." And blushed to the roots of her hair.

"Say it louder. You'll feel better."

She glanced around them, somewhat tempted, but she knew her limits. "No. I couldn't possibly."

"No one here knows you."

"It's not… No. I don't talk like that. I don't use those words."

He leaned forward. "All right, then. But nothing to stop you from shouting it at home. I swear it will help."

His cheer was infectious. She caught the fever. Bent closer. "I very well might." And giggled.

Giggled. Amazing.

He laughed, and she joined him. For a moment, the world seemed bright. Possible.

"Eat," he urged. "Please."

"You're a nice man," she said.

"Ouch. That's too much like *I think of you as a friend.*"

"Actually, I might." The admission surprised her.

"Well, double ouch. You know no man on earth wants to be considered a nice guy, don't you?" His eyes twinkled.

"That's too bad. Deal with it." Had she ever felt this playful? She picked up her burger, still hungry.

"Only if you promise you'll meet me again. The least you can do after insulting my manhood."

She'd had no real boyfriends before Hilton and little experience since then with flirting, but that was what this felt like, flirting with an interesting and very attractive man. Her insides were fluttery the way a teenage girl's might be, and it was a nice change from living in a constant cloud of gloom.

But it wouldn't do to get carried away. The gloom was real, and she couldn't afford distractions, even interesting and sexy ones.

Sexy. Had she really thought that? Sex was the absolute last thing on her mind. She was still technically married, for one thing.

If things were different, though…

They were not. Still, having a friend was a real comfort. She hadn't known him that long, but she liked what she knew of him thus far.

And she might have more questions. Definitely would, actually. He'd explained things in terms she could understand and hadn't made her feel like an idiot in the process. He wanted to help, and she didn't exactly have the luxury of rejecting it.

But that was as far as this could go. Anyway, it was she who was thinking of sex and attraction, not him. He'd probably turn tail and run.

I thought you were stunning. Wow. She would be remembering that for a long time.

Don't get ahead of yourself, missy. Living in fantasy is what got you in this fix.

But Gerty liked him, too. Had pleaded his cause.

"I'll consider meeting you again."

"Not good enough. You have to at least promise to take my calls. Or call me if you need something."

She tried to frown at him but couldn't quite manage. Anyway, what could a phone call hurt? He was a busy man; he wasn't likely to have a lot of time to chat on the phone.

"All right. I'll take your calls."

"Good." His eyes gleamed with satisfaction. "Now finish your meal."

"You're quite overbearing, you know that?"

"And proud of it, sweetcakes."

Sweetcakes. Maeve laughed. Amazing.

MAEVE SWITCHED OFF the television, elated. The Kansas race was over, and both her sons had finished without incident. According to the points standings in the Chase for the NASCAR Sprint Cup given by the announcers, Will had gained two spots to ninth, and Bart hadn't lost any, still sixth.

She was sure they were both chafing about not winning—every driver wanted to win every race, or they wouldn't have risen to be the top forty-three drivers in the world—but their finishes were respectable, and best of all, neither was out of contention, though Will's margin was on the edge.

She needed to be with them. Sure, they had girlfriends, however they each seemed to have a revolving cast, and there were teammates to support them, as well, but no one loved them as unconditionally as she did. And now, after everything that had happened with their father, maybe they needed to have that love reinforced.

So she would go to Talladega next Thursday and be there for them. She would cook good meals for them and just generally give them a mother's TLC. Now that they were older, they didn't seem to mind a little coddling now and again—they'd resisted firmly when they were first making the break to live on their own.

She had no desire to smother either of them. She was proud of their independence and the fine men they'd grown up to be. But she was a mother, and the only reliable parent they had.

Talladega always made her heart stop, the drafting that was essential to success but bunched the cars running at high speeds within inches of each other, creating the perfect storm for one mistake, one blown tire, one overheated engine to take out a dozen cars in an instant.

When she watched Talladega, a part of her wanted to cover her eyes and not look. It would be easy to postpone her return to the circuit for one more week—but that was all the more reason she must not. She had to be there for her boys, it was that simple.

The phone rang, and she almost didn't answer it, but she suspected it might be Chuck. She hadn't met him anywhere since the diner, but somehow they'd wound up talking every day, most often late at night when his work was done.

It wasn't late yet, but she'd talked enough about Bart and Will that Chuck understood some basics of NASCAR now. He also understood how crucial the Chase for the NASCAR Sprint Cup was to her sons' futures, with the need to impress the sponsors they'd had to struggle to find when their father's sponsorship, like so much else they'd counted on, had vanished.

"Hello?"

"Am I right in thinking that if Bart's pit crew hadn't blown that one stop, he could have won that race?" Chuck asked.

"They'll be doing extra practice this week, that's for sure." Then she smiled. "How are you, Chuck?"

"You don't want to talk about the race?"

"Of course I do, but I don't want to bore you." Then she had to ask. "Did you actually watch the whole thing?"

"I did."

"That's amazing. What did you think? Have you ever watched one before?"

"No, but it won't be the last one for me." He chuckled. "I love sports, and I can't think why I've never gotten into NASCAR before. There's still so much I have to learn, but it's a lot more interesting than I thought."

"It is. People who don't like it haven't really paid

attention. There's so much strategy involved, and luck plays a huge part, as well. But watching it on television is nothing compared to being at the track. I've never experienced anything like it."

"I'd like to catch a race sometime. Maybe you'd be my guide?"

"That might be fun…"

"I hear a *but* coming."

"Not really. I'm just thinking about next weekend. I'm going back to the track for the first time."

"You don't sound excited."

"I am…well, I'm not. I mean, I want to be there for the boys, and I used to enjoy the excitement of race weekends, but…"

"But you're worried. That's a lot of people. A lot of media."

"Yes, I do dread that, but I can stay tucked away from the limelight, and I'd guess their PR people will help with that. None of us wants my sons to be distracted, not at this critical time. I'm honestly not sure I'm doing the right thing by going, but they really want me there."

"Would you like company?"

She froze. An actual chill ran over her skin, and she couldn't decide if it was excitement or fear. Or both.

"I guess not," he said.

"No, that's not…" She didn't know what she thought. How would seeing her with a man affect her sons? What if other people noticed them together?

Not that they would be *together* together, of course. Not a couple, just…friends.

"I can practically hear your brain clicking, Maeve. This doesn't have to be hard. Just say, 'No, Chuck, I don't want you there.'"

In the numerous conversations they'd had since the diner, she'd enjoyed herself more than she could have imagined. He was extremely intelligent, frank, kind and sometimes funny. He was excellent company, and he was a comfort to her.

Not that he felt safe, exactly. She was too aware of him as a man for that.

"It's not that I—"

"Maeve, you have got to quit being so damn diplomatic all the time. Speak your mind, woman. How are you going to get out in the world and kick ass if you keep pussyfooting around the tough issues?"

"Okay, now you're making me angry."

"Good. Spit it out. Do you want me to go to Talladega with you or not?"

"It's not that simple."

"Sweetcakes, you could make a man crazy."

"I am not a sweetcakes," she responded. "That's demeaning."

He shouted with laughter. "It's a term of affection, Maeve, not an insult. What would you rather I call you—*honey bun?* How about *sugar pie?*" From his tone it was clear that he was ribbing her because she'd fallen back into what he called her princess-to-peasant mode.

Maeve gave up and laughed. "All right, all right. Sweetcakes it is." Term of affection, though? She'd have to think about that later. "So here's the unvarnished truth, *honey lamb*." She made her voice drip with Southern-fried charm.

Over his laughter, she continued. "I really want to be there for my boys, but I am not looking forward one bit to seeing all those people who only knew me as Hilton's wife. All the pity, the glances, the gossip. I dread it so much."

"Then let me accompany you. We can fly over in my plane. If it gets to be too much, I can fly you right back out."

"No. I made a promise to be there for the weekend, and I will stick it out."

"Good for you."

"Easy for you to say. But my being seen with another man when I'm not yet divorced, as well as my sons distracted by wondering what's going on between us, even though nothing is, well…I just can't risk it. They have too much on the line."

"So that's a no, then?"

She felt honest regret when she had to answer, "I think it has to be. But thank you, Chuck, truly. You don't know how tempting your offer is."

"Then make it up to me," he said.

"What?" She stifled her outrage. Didn't he understand—

"Let me take you to dinner this week. La Mireille. I'll get us a table in the vault so no one will bother you."

La Mireille was extravagantly expensive, an epicurean's dream of superb food and excellent service. It had once been a bank building, and the vault was used now for a single table where you could dine in privacy.

They would be alone but for the wait staff. The notion of that intimacy gave her the jitters. "You can't get the vault on this short notice. It's booked up for weeks."

"I can and I will, Maeve. Don't doubt it." The adventurer and captain of industry was speaking now.

She didn't doubt him. She just wasn't sure she dared accept. "I'll agree to dinner, but not there."

"You're being stubborn, Maeve, and for no reason. You want your privacy, and that's the best place to have it, short of coming to my house or me coming to yours."

She was definitely not ready for either. Perhaps she was making too much of this. He hadn't made a move on her, had been nothing but friendly with her. And he'd continued to help her with the financial homework she'd assigned herself. "Oh, all right."

"Don't sound so peeved. It's not ladylike." The humor was back in his voice.

"You are incorrigible, Mr. Lawrence."

"Yes, Princess, I am."

A smile crept past her confusion. She rolled her eyes. "When did you want to have this dinner?"

"When are you free?"

If she wasn't a lady she would have snorted. "I'm

free every night, Chuck, as you well know. One benefit of being a recluse."

"When do you leave for Talladega?"

"Thursday."

"How about Tuesday, then? Pick you up at seven?"

"I can—"

"If you tell me you can meet me there, sweet-cakes, I might just have to scream like a little girl."

The image was too much, the big, strapping man shrieking. Maeve started laughing. "That might be worth it."

"I love hearing you laugh, Maeve. I intend to do my best to see that it happens more often."

She sobered. "You're such a nice—" She didn't get to finish because a decidedly high-pitched noise, as close to a scream as his deep voice could manage, interrupted.

She was still laughing as she hung up the phone.

CHAPTER SEVEN

HE SHOWED UP with bird of paradise mingled with orchids.

She had on a simple black dress that was loose on her. He would have to do something about that. She needed to eat more.

Sweet heaven, her legs were killer hot.

It wasn't often that Chuck Lawrence found himself speechless, but the connection between eye and brain seemed to have short-circuited.

"These are gorgeous," she said, accepting the bouquet. "So unusual." Her cheeks were pink as she stroked a blossom, and he noticed, not for the first time, how delicate her fingers were. Couldn't help picturing them on his skin.

"Let me put them in water," she said, and turned. "I'll just be a minute."

The view of her from the back was just as good, trim ankles, shapely calves, shapely thighs leading up to a very nicely rounded—

"Chuck?" She bit her lower lip, another spot he didn't need to be thinking about. "Would you like to come inside?"

Get a grip, son. He realized he was still standing on the threshold like some kind of zombie. "Uh, yeah. Sure."

"Come on back. If you want to, that is." She passed out of the enormous open living area with its vaulted ceiling and through an equally impressive dining room he recalled from before.

He followed, not focusing on anything but her.

How had he ever thought her icy? Right now, closing the gap between them, he let his gaze travel up her back—okay, so it dipped now and again to those amazing legs—to where she'd swept her hair up and bared her nape.

He wanted to kiss her right there. He could nearly feel her smooth skin on his lips. His hands would be busy elsewhere. Everywhere. Mother of—

He shook his head, hoping to knock some sense into himself, but then his gaze fell to her legs again. Her heels weren't stilettos, but they still did that high-heeled magic with a woman's legs and derriere…

He was a leg man. Always had been. And Maeve Branch had some legs on her. His only excuse for not realizing that earlier was that she'd only worn jeans when he'd seen her this time around, and before, well, if you wanted to do business with a man—or even just consider it—you didn't scope out the man's wife.

He'd thought he only meant to help a woman in distress through a rough time. Be her friend. Smooth the waters wherever he could.

You're a nice man, she'd said.

Woman, you might not want to count on that, he thought now. He wasn't a bad person, no. He always tried to be aboveboard in his dealings with others, but he never hesitated to close in for the kill when needed. You didn't survive in the jungle of high-stakes risk without being willing to go for the win.

He meant her well and he would go easy on her, give her time, gentle her as he would a skittish mare. Do everything possible to shield her and guide her through this storm. The woman he'd felt sorry for, he'd discovered he admired, too. And he liked her, genuinely liked her.

But now he wanted her.

And what Chuck Lawrence wanted...he always—*always*—found a way to have.

CHUCK WAS MAKING her nervous, and she was uneasy enough already. Her dress didn't really fit, but she couldn't afford to buy a new one now. She'd gone through her closet—thank God he wouldn't get upstairs to see the disaster that was her bedroom. She no longer slept in the master bedroom but in the guest room she'd adopted as her own after Hilton's betrayal had come to light. She'd have to spend an hour tonight after she got home straightening the mess, but she'd panicked once she'd seen that nothing, absolutely nothing, fit—and then she'd run out of time.

It was bad enough to have to go out in public to such a visible place, but to do so poorly dressed was killing her. She hadn't even gotten there and she was already feeling sick to her stomach.

She hadn't realized how much she was counting on Chuck to be steady as always, to tease her and make her nerves go away. Now he was acting oddly, and her agitation increased.

Her fingers trembled as she tried to arrange the blossoms—how extraordinary, this choice, instead of the classic roses. Seeing them had made her feel… special.

But the way Chuck was looking at her, saying so little, she wasn't sure what to think.

Then he strode into her kitchen and…prowled. He had a gleam in his eye, too. She'd never felt anything like it, the way the atmosphere practically crackled. "You're making me nervous," she said. "Is something wrong?" She glanced down. "My dress isn't right. Nothing I have fits. Maybe we shouldn't—"

One dark eyebrow lifted. "You're not trying to weasel out, are you now, Maeve?" A slow, wicked smile curved his lips. "Because you promised. I don't think you take promises lightly." His head angled. "I don't. I definitely don't."

"But—" She stopped herself. She desperately needed to be brave.

If only it weren't so hard! All her life she'd found it miserable to be in the limelight, even when the attention was favorable. Being at the center of this circus, knowing people were clucking their tongues over her, *oh, that poor Maeve.* All those women, some of them old classmates at Hockaday, so sure of themselves, when she found it difficult even to answer a question in class, much less duel on the social stage. They grew up to be Amazons, striding out into the world fiercely— the way she never could. Their sly grins. *Can you imagine? Of course, she was always such a mouse.* Their glee. What had she ever done to deserve this?

You hid. You took the easy way out. And look what it gained you.

She must, once again, force herself out into society as she had so often when Hilton demanded it. She had done it to keep peace and, if she was honest, to buy the time alone with her babies. All it had cost her was her family's heritage and her own self-respect.

So she would come out of hiding, no matter how badly she wanted to stay burrowed.

But this time, she would be doing it as the first step, as tentative as a new filly's, in figuring out who she would become.

"All right," she said, giving the blossoms one last stroke. Forcing herself ramrod straight when she wanted to crumple. "Let me get my purse."

"Attagirl." Chuck nodded. "I'm proud of you, Maeve."

She ascended the stairs with her insides quaking.

But feeling just a little taller. And a tiny bit proud of herself.

THE CLOSER THEY GOT, the paler she became. Her knees were locked together, her back straight as a ruler in a pose that she'd probably learned as soon as she could walk.

She'd laced her fingers together so tightly in her lap her knuckles were white. She no longer seemed frosty or superior—he'd been blind to think so when they'd first met. She was the shyest of violets, he was learning, thriving best when nestled deep in a woodland glade. Being forced into the harsh glare that was Hilton Branch's showboating ways must have been excruciating.

He pulled up to the valet parking stand, and as an attendant in crisp white shirt, black pants, vest and tie rounded the hood, Chuck leaned toward Maeve. "I won't leave your side."

Her face was a mask. "I'm fine," she insisted.

How many times in her life had she said that to someone, whistling past the graveyard?

"I know you are," he responded, though she was clearly anything but. He squeezed one of the tightly clasped hands just as both their doors were being opened, and a second attendant helped Maeve out, though Chuck had wanted to do the honor.

He quickly rounded the back of the car and approached her, handing off the keys to the sedan he seldom drove. He took Maeve's hand and tucked it under his arm. "I hope you appreciate that I drove the sedate car," he said to her, "instead of my pickup."

She flashed him a startled but, he thought, grateful smile for the distraction. "I'm not sure something this snazzy counts as 'sedate'."

"Of course it does." He grinned at her. "My wife was not a fan of pickups. She never understood that you can take the boy out of the country, but the country never leaves the boy."

"She must not have grown up in Texas."

He shook his head. "Connecticut."

"Poor thing," she said. "Some men's pickups cost the earth." Then she smiled faintly. "Like yours, I imagine."

He shrugged. "Boys need their toys."

Her smile this time was genuine, and for a second, he was tempted to whisk her right out of this place and take her where it would be just the two of them.

But she needed to know she could manage this, so instead, he nodded at the maître d'.

"Mr. Lawrence, it is a pleasure, as always." The man turned to Maeve. "Mrs. Branch, it is good to see you again."

To her credit, Maeve was as poised and gracious as a queen. "Thank you, Leonard."

"This way, please. Your table is waiting."

Chuck felt Maeve's hand clench, just for a second, on his arm. He cast about for some subtle way to reassure her.

She beat him to it, releasing his arm, then straightened and followed Leonard, head high like the Dallas royalty she was. Avid faces swiveled her way, and more than one conversation ceased. Pity was much in evidence, greedy curiosity coming in a close second.

Chuck could almost feel her fear, but none of it was betrayed by her demeanor. She nodded here and there, her smile always cordial, and he thought that only he understood that it sprang not from the heart but from sheer courage.

He shook a hand here, made his own nods there, but he never lagged behind as he exchanged greetings with his fellow movers and shakers, focusing, instead, on staying as close to Maeve as he could without ruining her show of pure bravado.

When at last they entered the vault, he was surprised at the relief he felt that her ordeal was over— at least, until they had to depart. Nonetheless, she remained in character, chatting with the maître d' as he seated her, as though it was just any day, not her first real foray into the glaring light of public scrutiny.

He'd ordered champagne for them, and the bottle was already chilled and waiting. La Mireille didn't have menus; the chef decided each day what he would serve, and patrons chose from those options, but he would also prepare a meal to order. Knowing how nervous Maeve was likely to be and how little appetite she'd had lately, he'd chosen the meal in advance in consultation with Gerty—she now allowed him to call her that—so that it contained Maeve's favorites.

When the champagne had been tasted and poured, they were finally alone. The vault door remained open, of course, but a clever shield of wine racks and greenery had been devised so that other patrons could not peer inside. The space was lined with more wine bottles and a few choice pieces of art, the atmosphere made cozy and intimate by subdued soft-gold lighting while candles flickered atop the burgundy tablecloth. It was the perfect spot for a seduction to begin, though at the time he'd suggested it, Chuck hadn't had seducing Maeve on his mind.

He did now.

Except that Maeve looked as though she might faint at any second.

He lifted his flute. "To the bravest woman I know."

Her eyes filled, and her hand trembled as she set her flute down. "Not really." She stared at the wall in front of her, blinking hard. "I am so tired of weeping," she whispered. "Of feeling weak and scared."

If he'd ever admired a woman more, he wasn't sure when. Not since his mother had someone's courage impressed him so. He took her hand and wrapped it around the stem of her flute again. "One day at a time, Maeve. You're doing great." He lifted his champagne again and clinked it to hers.

She closed her eyes. "Thank you."

He saw the flutter of her pulse at her throat and he desired her, yes, more than he could have imagined, but he wanted to hug her, to hold her close even more. Protective instincts roared to life within him, and he knew that he wasn't going anywhere soon. "To Maeve," he said simply.

She lifted her lashes and met his gaze for long seconds. At last she raised her glass. "To friends."

She was nowhere near ready for seduction, he understood she was telling him. Perhaps she could be, though, if he was patient. He'd possessed almost no patience when he was younger, all fired up to grab life and wring all he could from it.

But the best things were worth waiting for, he'd learned, mostly the hard way.

"To friends," he agreed—for the time being, at least. Their flutes touched once more before they tasted the champagne.

"Mmm," Maeve said, and delicately licked a drop lingering on her lower lip. "That's lovely."

Chuck raked one hand through his hair and stifled a groan as he willed his suddenly unruly body into submission. He was not a young stud anymore, all brute strength and heat, but at the moment, he could sure remember being exactly that.

So, apparently, could his body.

Slow down, he willed himself. *Cool your jets, boy.*

He drank faster than a fine vintage like this should be drunk.

Then he looked at Maeve in the candle's glow and agreed, "Yes, lovely indeed."

He wondered if she realized that he was not referring to the champagne.

THE MEAL WAS DIVINE, the wine Chuck had chosen exquisite. And having a rugged, handsome, intriguing male across the table was no hardship.

If only she could stay in the cocoon he had created here, luxuriating in the stimulating conversation of a man whose beginnings had been much rougher than her own but who had carved out a life to admire. He was a fount of stories, and he told them with panache, tales of his fellow roughnecks, of the people among whom he'd grown up. Clever tales, too, of mutual acquaintances.

He was an interesting man, this Chuck Lawrence, mostly self-educated, yet he could discuss books and films, paintings and travel with all the aplomb of an Ivy League graduate. She found herself laughing often and forgetting, for a while, the lions' den outside through which she would have to pass when dinner was over.

But there were moments when she wasn't sure that all the lions were safely outside. Chuck's eyes took on a gleam when he looked at her that she had no idea how to handle.

He might be seated, but every once in a while, she had the sense that he was prowling again. That his prey might be her.

The idea was unsettling. Terrifying.

Thrilling.

She was not remotely ready to get involved with a man again—might never be. She'd probably mistaken his interest, anyway.

Just then, he looked up. "What?"

She gulped, then cast about for something to divert attention she found both exciting and unnerving. "Tell me something about your wife."

He frowned a little. "Why?"

Because I need the distance. Aloud she said, "The way you spoke of her and your pickup, you sounded as if you were close."

"Of course. We were married twenty-six years."

"The number of years together guarantees nothing." She arched one eyebrow. "Hilton and I were married for thirty-three."

"Touché," he said. "June and I were happy—at least, most of the time. Raising a family and building a business at the same time, you have rough spots. You work through them if the love is there." He paused. "Losing her…"

"I'm sorry. I shouldn't have asked."

He shook his head. "It's okay. I didn't date for a long time afterward. I just—I wasn't ready. Instead, I worked. The kids were happy, I think, that I didn't. No child wants to see a parent replaced, even if the child is grown. But after a while, they started trying to fix me up, and their idea of my taste…" He gave a mock shudder. "I had to begin asking women out just in self-defense."

"So is there someone special?" she asked, keeping her tone carefully light, unsure what she wanted his answer to be.

"I hadn't thought so." His gaze locked on hers.

Maeve couldn't help a small shiver of alarm. Of tantalizing possibility. She hastened to find another distraction. "Do your children live nearby?"

His eyes crinkled at the corners as if he understood exactly what she was doing. "No. Chad lives in Minnesota and is engaged to a lovely girl, a nurse. He's a marketing executive. Dan is in L.A., a sports agent who likes his bachelor life just fine." A wry grin. "But can't leave his old man to do the same."

Maeve chuckled. "Your daughter, where is she?"

"Lizzie, the light of my life. She's at Columbia, doing graduate work in art history. She looks just like her mother, more so every year."

They chatted together easily for a while longer, but soon it was impossible to ignore that the time to leave had come.

She seized the initiative, however much she dreaded what lay ahead. "Thank you, Chuck. This has been wonderful." She paused, mentally steeling herself. "We should go now."

His fond gaze was a caress. "Leonard will let us leave through the kitchen if you'd prefer."

That meant no promenade through avid glances, lifted brows. "Tempting." She summoned a smile. "But I have to face this."

"Good girl." He rose and assisted her with her chair. Clasped her arms with his hands and squeezed. "My car will be right outside the door when we get there."

She half turned to look at him, very aware that his

shoulders were broad, his body a shelter. His lips close…so close.

She risked one touch of his jaw. "Thank you, Sir Galahad." She smiled. "You're such—"

A tiny scream began to rise from his throat, and they both laughed.

"You weren't, of course, going to call me a nice man, right?"

Her voice took on the cadence of a Southern belle. "Why, Mr. Lawrence, how could you think that?"

A hand to the small of her back, he escorted her through the restaurant, chuckling. With him beside her, nothing seemed so bad. She was turning her face up to him to pose an impertinent question when the front door opened—

—And all hell broke loose outside.

Strobe lights popped like starbursts amid the harsh glare of television cameras, and voices clamored.

"Mrs. Branch, over here!"

"Maeve, have you heard…"

"What do you think about your husband's confession that he…"

Maeve froze in terror, blinded by the lights, dizzy from the assault.

Beside her, Chuck went into immediate action, shielding her with his body, sweeping her along and into the car so quickly everything blurred, barking orders at the restaurant staff as he rounded the hood and drove her away. In seconds, he had her out of there, his eyes constantly checking the rearview mirror where one van was following them.

Maeve felt glued to the leather seat, staring into the oncoming traffic but seeing nothing, her hands clasped as though that would keep her from shattering.

Chuck was on his cell, snapping out orders as he took evasive action, one quick turn after another. With a throaty roar, the powerful engine carried them down roads she didn't recognize. Chuck drove with easy confidence. "Hold on, sweetheart," he said, and laid one hand over hers.

The warmth of his skin crept into her flesh, sending a shudder through her body like hypothermia losing its grip. He looked over at her in concern. "Do you want the heater on?"

"No," she managed. "I just want to go home."

He flicked a glance in the rearview mirror. "We've lost them now. I don't think your house is a good idea. I have somewhere else in mind."

But she'd had too much. Of everything—people, noise, fear...even of him. He stirred too much in her, shook her in ways she wasn't ready for. She was accustomed to solitude, and right now she craved it like a drug.

"I need to be alone, Chuck."

"Maeve, I'm sorry that happened, but I assure you I will find out who's responsible and punish them. You did well tonight, but going back home... They could be waiting for you. Do you want to go through another gauntlet?"

He was the voice of reason, but she felt anything but reasonable right now. She felt stripped naked, exposed to the glare of other people's greed, their disregard for her privacy, for her pain, for the fear that lived with her, night and day. She had no idea where her life was headed or how she would manage, and she would make her mistakes, it appeared, on a very public stage. When she hit rock bottom, would they finally leave her alone? Was that what they were waiting for—her complete and final fall?

"Take me to Penny's, then." Abruptly, she remembered that Penny and Craig were out of town. "No, that won't work." She rubbed her forehead, casting about for a solution.

"Let me take you to my home, Maeve."

"No!" She knew her voice was too sharp, but she couldn't deal with that option, not right now. She was too attracted to him as a man, to the shelter he represented—and too uncertain which called to her the most.

At any rate, a relationship was the last thing she wanted right now.

"Where does Gerty live?" he asked quietly.

Relief whipped through her. She closed her eyes. Gerty was the perfect solution. She gave him directions.

Then gave him his due. "Thank you." She made herself face him. "I'm sorry. I wanted to be ready for this—" she fluttered a hand, as vague as she felt about what this might include "—but I'm not." *In-*

cluding you, she let her eyes speak the words she would not say.

Then she turned away, ashamed.

The rest of the trip proceeded in uncomfortable silence.

CHAPTER EIGHT

WHEN MAEVE DODGED his calls over the next two days before she left for Talladega, Chuck told himself he was better off. He had a good life, including Cecily Dunstan—a woman as uninterested in marriage as he was—when he wanted female companionship. He had plenty of challenges in business. He didn't need a complicated woman, especially not one as complicated as Maeve.

He'd found the source of the leak at La Mireille, a busboy who made money on the side tipping off reporters when interesting clientele showed up. That young man was now persona non grata at all the fine establishments in town. Chuck had gotten Maeve out of there and had turned her over to the tender care of Gerty, who'd been sympathetic to him each time he'd called, clearly uncomfortable with the white lies she'd been asked to tell him about why Maeve couldn't come to the phone.

He should be happy to dust his hands of her. He should be taking Cecily out for dinner or taking off to the lake to fish.

Instead, he was in his plane heading to Talladega for his first NASCAR race, having pulled some strings to get invited to the same suite where Maeve would be watching the event.

Holding some damn-fool notion of being nearby in case Maeve needed him.

His competitors would be laughing their butts off to see that hard-charging Chuck Lawrence, who never lost his cool in business—and almost never lost at anything, period—had apparently gone soft in the head over a woman who wouldn't even take his calls.

But what Maeve Branch didn't understand was that saying no to a man like himself was akin to waving raw meat in front of a hungry lion.

"GIDEON TANEY is such a nice man," Maeve said to her sons at the airport. Then the memory of Chuck Lawrence attempting a little-girl scream had her ducking her head to smother a smile.

But not quick enough. "What is it, Mom?" Bart asked, one arm around her shoulders. "What's so funny?"

"Nothing," she replied quickly. "Just a joke the pilot told me."

"You know we like jokes," Will responded. "Tell us."

"Surely you recall that I can't tell a joke to save my life." She sought refuge in banter. "And you like to pull pranks, the more complicated the better. Don't think I've forgotten." She smiled widely at her boys, stroking their cheeks. "I'm steeling myself."

"Mom, we would never—"

She arched a brow. "That innocent look only makes me more certain I'm in trouble."

"Honestly, Mom, after all you've been through," Bart said, "there's no way we would inflict a prank on you."

He meant it, she could tell. Will, too. "Then I owe you an even bigger apology than I thought. I have been a coward, and I'm ashamed of myself."

"Mom, don't you dare think that," Bart argued. "That bastard stole everything from you. Anyone would be thrown for a loop."

"Yeah," Will chimed in. "You are no coward. You're just—" he shrugged "—delicate."

"Oh, good grief. That sounds like someone who'd take to her fainting couch with the vapors."

Both of them chuckled. "Not really you, Mom."

"Frighteningly close, I'm afraid. I've been hiding, and someone has made me see how wrong that is."

"What someone?"

"Just…a friend." Though she hadn't been much of a friend in return, now had she?

"You okay, Mom?" Will asked.

She snapped back to the present. "Absolutely." She straightened, summoned a smile. "So, who am I staying with tonight?"

"Me," Bart said. "Will got to be the hero hooking you up with Taney's plane." He frowned slightly. "If

I still had mine, I'd put it at your disposal anytime. I'm so glad you're here, Mom."

Both sons had been given private jets by their father when they made it to the NASCAR Sprint Cup Series level—a typically flamboyant gesture from a man who specialized in them. When Hilton had disappeared and their sponsorships with him, the twins had each sold their planes to get money to help with team expenses until new sponsors had been found.

"Don't you worry a bit, sweetheart," she said. "I can fly commercial next time." If she cut enough corners to afford it, that was.

We can fly over in my plane, Chuck had offered. But she was not going to think about Chuck anymore. Or about how badly she'd let him down, panicking like that at La Mireille.

"You won't have to. Taney and Jim Latimer have each offered to help out whenever you'd like to attend a race." Bart paused. "Unless you want to come stay in Charlotte for a while and travel with the teams next time you're up for a race?"

"I won't be missing another one," she said, though her insides quivered a bit. She hadn't yet encountered anyone from NASCAR, much less the media, but she would not let her boys down again. "Watching you on television isn't the same. Besides, I think you need some of my cooking. You both look thin."

Wide grins flashed. "Yep, she's still Mom. 'You're too thin, boys,'" Will mocked her in falsetto. "'Better let me feed you.'"

"Well, you are," she insisted, grinning right back. "Let's stop at the grocery store on the way to the track."

"Yes!" Bart pumped a fist while Will hugged her. "Mom's back."

Arm in arm, they made their way to the parking lot.

WHO YOU KNOW is every bit as important as what you know. That lesson had been drummed into Chuck's head by the man who'd first agreed to joint-venture a real-estate deal with him, a run-down apartment house in East Dallas where his business partner, Joe Sayers, had provided the down payment and Chuck had contributed the sweat equity.

They'd gone on to do a couple more deals together before Joe passed away, and Chuck had learned more from that old man than simple business practices, things like a code of honor that echoed the way Chuck's mother had raised him. Some people believed honor was out of date in today's business world—hell, in the world in general—but Chuck disagreed. A man's word should be his bond, cradle to grave. Yes, you needed lawyers to put agreements on paper, but if the honor wasn't there, the weightiest contract was worth less than the paper it was printed on. You could always find a lawyer willing to seek out wiggle room if you wanted to welsh on a deal. In the end, a man's character was all you could truly count on.

Through Joe, Chuck had met other businessmen

who lived by that code. One such man had been Richard Latimer, the recently deceased owner of PDQ Racing, Bart Branch's team. The older man was a gentleman of the old school, and a philanthropist, as well. Chuck had served with Richard on a couple of boards, and the two men had become friends.

Richard's nephew and heir, Jim, whom Chuck had met several times, had been happy to invite Chuck to join them in their suite.

The same suite where Maeve would be watching the race.

The sight greeting Chuck as the helicopter he'd chartered from the airport circled the superspeedway was something to behold. He'd attended Super Bowls and NCAA Final Fours, the NBA Finals and the World Series with all their hoopla, but he'd never witnessed anything like this.

The campers and tents went on forever. Actually, a great number of them appeared to be in their cars, clogging the roads for miles back, or walking from great distances where they'd parked, streaming into the race track.

Which was one astonishing sight in itself. "There are the grandstand seats, plus all those folks camped out in the infield. There's the drivers' and owners' lot." The pilot pointed. "It has a security fence to keep out the women—at least, the unwanted ones."

"Unwanted women?" Chuck asked.

"Ones on the prowl for drivers. If these boys were

rock stars, those ladies would be the groupies tossing their underwear on the stage."

"Ah," Chuck said. "I get the picture."

"You want a picture, you go out and wander the campgrounds. Talladega is a week-long party. Folks with families camp separate from the rowdy crowd." The man shrugged. "People come here year after year, got their own communities built up—people they see only twice a year at the races but who might as well be family. That's the NASCAR Nation, however outsiders might misunderstand it—one big family, sometimes happy, sometimes fussing and feuding, but united by their love of the sport."

Maeve had said something similar once. "It's absolutely amazing. Has to be seen to be believed."

"This your first time at this track?"

"My first race."

The man chuckled. "Well, sir, you have got yourself one big surprise in store. You sitting in the stands or up in a suite?"

"A suite."

The pilot shook his head. "Not the right way to experience racing. You want to understand the sport, you need to rub elbows with the crowd. Smell the fumes, hear those engines roar. Nothing like it. Been a fan since I was a kid, and I still get goose bumps when the green flag drops."

"I'll have to try that next time," Chuck said. Though there might not be a next time; he was here for Maeve and had no idea what he would think about the race itself. The pageant of color he could see below him as they headed for the landing zone was amazing—the colors of the team uniforms, the fans seemingly all in driver regalia, the cars themselves. He experienced a little of the feeling he'd had as a kid the one time he won a contest for selling newspaper subscriptions and went to the circus. He'd fallen head over heels with the spectacle of it.

Then they were landing, and the time for conversation was done. "Thank you," Chuck said, and handed the man a generous tip. Then he paused in the doorway, "Who are you rooting for?"

"Who's your driver—that's how you ask it." The pilot paused. "I've been a Dean Grosso man from way back when, but he's gonna be retiring soon, I bet, so I've been watching his son, Kent, the reigning champion. I kinda like those Branch twins, too. Boys are hotheaded, especially that Will, but they sure got talent. Drive the wheels right off."

Chuck grinned. Children of gentle Maeve's with a temper—this he'd have to see. He nearly offered to get the pilot an autograph but realized that he was getting ahead of himself. "You have a card?"

"Sure thing." The pilot handed him a business card. "You booked with us after the race?"

"No," Chuck replied. "I'm not sure how soon I'll be leaving." Much would depend on Maeve's reaction to his presence.

But if things worked out, he would at least see about getting the pilot some souvenirs from Maeve's hotheaded boys.

"I WAS SO VERY SORRY to hear about Richard," Maeve said to Jim Latimer, the new owner of Bart's team, PDQ Racing. "I apologize for missing the funeral."

"The flowers you sent were much appreciated," the younger man said as he escorted her beneath the grandstands toward the elevator that led to the suites. "You've had your own worries."

Maeve couldn't help flinching inwardly at even the most oblique reference to Hilton's betrayal. "You had them, too—losing your uncle and working with new sponsors, as well. I cannot begin to tell you how sorry I am for what Hilton did." Shame made her chest tight.

"Mrs. Branch—"

"Maeve, please." She could barely stand to hear that last name in relation to herself. Were it not for her children, she'd change it the second the divorce was final.

"Maeve, then." He swung to face her, drew her to the side as the elevator door opened, so that others couldn't hear. "You are the victim in this much more than anyone else. None of us expected his actions—and absolutely no one blames you."

She couldn't meet his gaze. "Unless they've read that woman's book." Alyssa Ritchie had claimed that Hilton came to her because he couldn't get what he needed at home. That he'd told her how he suffered from being married to a cold woman who only cared about his money—never mind that she'd been the one with the money when they'd married. Her children had tried to keep the book from her, but she'd been desperate to know what was being said, however painful it might be, and Gerty had finally agreed to get a copy when Maeve insisted.

Some days she wished she could tear out every shred of memory of that woman's vile accusations.

She was not cold—except on the inside, in that small place where a girl once dreamed of a great love. Maeve had had to draw her comfort from her children's affection, instead, being so very careful not to depend on them too much. It was not a child's duty to make up for a husband's lack.

"No one with any sense gives that tramp a shred of credibility," Jim Latimer said, his voice kind.

"Some people enjoy gossip a great deal, Mr. Latimer."

"Jim. And some people are idiots."

"You're a lovely man, Jim," she said. "Richard was right to be proud of you." She pulled herself very straight. "I'm keeping you from your guests."

"Don't be nervous, Maeve. You are my most honored guest. I'd be pleased if you'd sit with my family." He flashed a grin. "Even though Bart tells me you have to root for Will this time."

Her case of nerves eased slightly. "My boys don't seem to understand that a mother cannot possibly choose between her children. They came up with that system years ago, knowing I have a soft spot for the underdog, and I played along because it helped stave off chaos with two very competitive little boys."

"Who've grown up to be two very competitive men."

She nodded. "But best friends, as well." She couldn't help a little sigh. "If only one of them had preferred soccer or basketball or something."

Jim chuckled. "I have a hard enough time raising one boy, and you had three, plus a daughter." He sketched a bow. "I might need to put your phone number on speed dial. Your kids have all turned out to be terrific people."

He was right; she did have wonderful children—and it was time for her to support them. "Thank you for that." She took his arm. "Let's go watch a race."

He patted her hand and escorted her upstairs. He was the soul of solicitude, introducing her to those in their path inside the suite but seeming to understand that she wasn't up for a lot of chitchat, quickly leading her over to where his new wife Anita, Bart's public relations rep, and his eight-year-old son, Billy, sat. She was surprised to see the boy, since children weren't normally permitted in the suites where alcohol was served. Anita explained that as a widowed single father with a son who needed him, when Jim had been thrust into ownership of the team, he hadn't wanted Billy excluded and thus had pulled some strings to have the serving of alcohol prohibited in PDQ's suite.

Once Billy discovered that she was Bart's mother, he had a steady stream of questions. Bart was his hero, and Billy had aspirations of being a driver. He wanted to know everything possible about Bart as a boy, and Maeve found herself relaxing. However much her world had become a frightening and unfamiliar place, she understood children and enjoyed their company.

Anita excused herself to join Jim in greeting guests, offering to get Maeve a plate of food from the buffet, but Maeve was too nervous to eat. Billy was hungry, though, so he left her, promising to come back as soon as he'd filled his plate.

Even in what she thought of now as the good old days, she'd found herself unable to eat before a race. She had spent every race since her boys had begun competing whispering prayers that they not be hurt.

So Maeve stayed right where she was, alone on the front row of seats in the box, off in the far right corner, staring down at the track to her sons' pit boxes. Will had qualified fifteenth and Bart sixth. Both crew chiefs had offered to let her sit up with them, and Maeve's suite pass would allow her to do so, but she never felt that she had a real handle on the big picture from down there. She needed to watch her boys every second, not just when they roared by. In the suites, the backstretch, too, was visible.

Part of her understood that a rational person would say she didn't really have the power to keep them safe by paying total attention, but motherhood was not a wholly rational experience. Logic and a mother's love fought a constant battle, and somewhere deep inside, Maeve believed that her fierce love would make the difference. Her sons would soon be attaining very high speeds with cars bunched mere inches apart. If the force of her will could serve as a shield around them, then how could she not try?

"You need to eat, Maeve," said a very familiar voice.

Her head jerked up. "Chuck?" She rose abruptly from her chair. "What are you doing here?" She backed up a step and nearly lost her balance.

Chuck grabbed her before she could fall. "I didn't mean to startle you." He held on to her arms, staring down at her. "You looked…lonely."

"But—" she shook her head "—how…" She blinked. "You said you don't attend races."

"I said I hadn't yet. I was hoping to go with you the first time, but—" a shrug "—you didn't want me to come."

Was that a faint stab of hurt she saw? Surely not. "So why are you here?"

"You want the truth or a polite fiction?" His gaze was intense, and she was incredibly aware of him.

"I'm not sure."

"Well, you get the truth. I was worried about you, been worried about you every blessed hour since you made me leave you at Gerty's. But you won't take my calls. Treat me like some damn stalker." His voice was rising in volume, and she watched him struggle to modulate it. He released her and stepped back. "You were dreading being here, and after what happened the other night…" His look was pure chagrin. "I find myself in the position of being unable to leave you to the wolves, however stupid that makes me."

"You all right, Maeve?" Jim appeared by her side. "Chuck?"

"Yeah," Chuck said, his voice rough. "If you'll excuse me." He turned and walked away.

"Maeve? Is there a problem? Chuck and my father were good friends, served on a couple of boards together, so when he asked if there was room, I was happy to say yes, but I never realized…"

Maeve was staring at Chuck's retreating broad back, uncertain how to feel.

"I'll ask him to go." Jim made to leave.

"No!" Maeve grabbed his arm. "No, Jim, it's not what you think." She angled her head. "He's here—" she found herself more moved than she wanted to be "—to protect me." Her insides were scrambled, and her boys were about to race. She didn't want to be distracted by Chuck, but hadn't she been rude enough to a man who'd done nothing to deserve it?

"Really?"

She looked at Jim, at the confusion in his eyes. Felt its echo in her. She lifted her hands. "I seem to have acquired a champion, though I have no idea why."

Jim smiled. "I do. You're one hell of a woman, Maeve Branch." He bent lower and whispered, "But don't tell my wife." He chuckled.

She smiled right back, until she realized Chuck was leaving. "Do not say a word to my boys, please.

Chuck and I are just friends. I don't want to upset them, especially not during the Chase."

"Mum's the word," Jim said.

Maeve barely heard, already climbing the steps in pursuit of Chuck. She heard the announcer say that the driver introductions were about to begin, and she muttered an unladylike curse beneath her breath. She didn't want to miss a second of her boys' moments in the sun—but she was not a rude woman by nature, and she had amends to make. She darted out the suite door and saw Chuck striding down the abandoned corridor, headed toward the elevator.

"Chuck! Wait!"

He halted. Squared his shoulders, shook his head and finally turned.

She skidded to a stop before him. "I'm sorry. I'm rude and awful when you've been nothing but kind, and you can yell at me if you want." She grabbed his hand and started towing him back toward the suite, which was a little bit like trying to move a mountain.

"Come on," she said. "I have to get back right now."

"What about the yelling?"

"You'll have to wait until the race is over. Now hurry up! They're about to introduce my sons." She dropped his hand and began running.

He caught up with her quickly, grasped her hand and lent his own strength to the task of closing the distance. At the door, he halted her before she yanked the door open. "If you don't want to be the center of attention, you might want to slow down."

Her chest heaving from the unaccustomed exertion, Maeve tried to catch her breath and nodded. She smoothed her hair, straightened her clothes, then surprised herself by rising on her toes and pressing one quick kiss to his cheek. "I'm sorry. And thank you."

Then she was through the door, her gaze fastened only on the stage where her sons would soon appear.

CHAPTER NINE

"I'M SO THRILLED for Will—finishing fourth, plus getting five bonus points for leading a lap, puts him up to seventh in the points," Maeve said to Chuck as the race ended. "But poor Bart will be so unhappy, even though he pulled off a miracle after that accident, fighting his way back up to eleventh. All he'll focus on is dropping in the points from sixth to eighth, and falling behind his brother. Oh, that will vex him."

"Vex?" Chuck teased. "That's what he'd say right about now?"

She cut a reproving glance at him, but Anita Latimer answered first. "If he uses language that mild to the press, I'll be thrilled. A penalty could come back to haunt him." She clasped Billy's hand. "Let's find your father, so I can go save Bart from himself." Jim Latimer had left the suite after the first few laps, headed for the pit box. He liked his team to know he was there for them.

"But I want to see Bart, too," Billy protested.

"Would you like to walk down with us, Billy?"

Maeve asked. "I'll be meeting up with him at his motor home once Anita is through helping him."

Anita was clearly relieved, but the boy looked doubtful. "I don't want to miss him."

"Neither do I," Maeve responded. "And we won't—but Anita needs to get there first." When Billy continued to seem hesitant, Maeve bent down. "Would you like to hear about the time the twins switched classes and fooled their teachers?"

Billy's eyes lit up. "Sure!"

"You go ahead," Maeve told Anita.

"Thank you so much, Maeve." Anita turned back toward Chuck. "Here are some credentials so the guards will let you into the infield."

"Thanks," he replied.

"See you all down there." Anita broke into a run and soon disappeared from sight.

Chuck watched as Maeve regaled Billy with more stories about her boys while leading the way down to the tunnel that connected the stands to the infield. Her love of children was obvious. She must have been one hell of a mother.

Beneath the stands, they joined the throngs, and he marveled again at the sheer number of fans, as well as at how smoothly the traffic flowed out the exits. Everywhere he looked, people wore the gear of their favorite drivers. In his golf shirt and jeans, he was a fish out of water—but Maeve was, too, if judged by her lack of driver gear. She would, of course, face a real conflict trying to dress equally for both sons, so she'd apparently chosen to wear the attire of neither. Her outfit was simple and unpretentious, but those killer legs were visible below the hem of her denim skirt, and following her as he was, he had a nice view of her hips. Hips he'd like to get his hands on.

He frowned. Her clothing still hung on her, and he'd spotted the shadows beneath her eyes. She wasn't sleeping or eating well, he was certain, and he wondered how much the events at La Mireille had harmed her.

But at the moment, her eyes sparkled as she conversed with the boy. And she'd kissed his cheek. Did that mean he was forgiven?

He noted Billy lagging and drew closer, then bent down. "Want a ride, Billy?"

"Sure!"

"Turn around." Chuck grasped the boy under his arms and lifted him to his shoulders.

"Cool! I can see over everybody," Billy declared exultantly.

Chuck was happy to help the boy out, but it was the appreciative, maybe even admiring look he got from Maeve that made him feel best. A lot of his contemporaries had let their physical conditioning slide as they aged, but he kept to a rigorous workout schedule, and at the moment, he was very glad. "Lead on, madam," he said to Maeve, holding onto the boy's ankles.

"This way," she responded. "So tell me what you

thought of the race," she asked as they threaded through the crowd.

"I didn't expect it to be so exciting. There's too much I don't understand—" he cast her a glance "—but I'm hoping you're up for questions later."

Her gaze was at once shy and a little eager. "I just might be," she said, then returned her attention to their path. "Here we are." After passing the guard, she led them through the tunnel and out into the infield. She began to point out the sights. "There's pit road, and the garages are over that way."

"Where will your sons be?"

"Will has to go to the media center. The top five finishers are always expected to be there for interviews after the race." Her forehead wrinkled. "Bart will likely head straight for his motor home. He'll want to brood, and he'll say I should leave him alone, but he seldom means it. He'll be surly as a wounded bear, but I'll take my chances, just in case he needs to talk." She glanced up at Billy. "Let me go see him first, all right? Find out if he's up for company?"

"Okay," Billy replied. "Tell him I still think he's great, and I know Dad does, too."

"I absolutely will." She smiled. "Thank you."

Chuck patted the boy's leg. "We'll come with you, but remain outside until you call us."

They began to move again toward the guard at the entrance to the drivers' and owners' lot, but just as they arrived, someone with a camera spotted Maeve. "Mrs. Branch!" he shouted, snapping pictures as fast as his motor drive would go. "Have you seen your husband yet? Did he tell you what he did with the money?" He began to race toward them, and another photographer joined him.

Maeve looked like a deer caught in headlights. Chuck grasped her arm and towed her to the security guard.

"Here," he told the man. "They both have credentials. Get them inside." He lowered Billy to the ground and hustled him and Maeve inside the gate.

Then he turned and glared at the two men. "Get back, or I'll move you myself." When one of them kept snapping shots, he shoved the telephoto lens toward the ground. Rage seared through him. He advanced on them.

"You can't do this," one of them said. "You have no right. Ever heard of freedom of the press?"

"Have you ever heard of harassment? Or assault?"

"I never touched her," said the other.

"We're just trying to get a story," said the first.

"She's not the criminal here. Beat it." Chuck got in their faces. "Or I will devote my last dime to making you sorry you didn't."

First one, then the second camera trained on him and began snapping. "Our lawyers will be all over you. What's your name?"

"I'm not afraid of your lawyers," Chuck said, his tone full of menace. "And you're the press, you figure out who I am. Now get lost." He advanced on them again, and they finally broke ranks and took off, throwing curse words in his direction. Chuck stood in place until they were out of sight.

"Good work," said the security guard. "I was going to help, but you had it all under control."

"Who the hell are you?" said a new voice off to one side.

Chuck wheeled, ready to do battle until he recognized the face of Bart Branch, still in his uniform. Outside the lot, not in. "A friend of your mother's. Chuck Lawrence," he said, extending a hand.

"I've never heard her mention you," Bart said suspiciously, though he shook hands. "But thanks for what you just did. I'm Bart."

"I know. I sat with your mother in PDQ's suite. She's in the lot now with Billy, looking for you. Nice job of making it back to the front."

True to Maeve's prediction, Bart scowled. "Hardly the front. I lost two spots in the Chase today, thanks to a stupid driver who should go back to racing go-karts."

"She said you'd be vexed."

Bart's head jerked up. "Vexed?"

Chuck grinned. "Anita catch you before you could say something worse?"

"I certainly did," came Anita's voice from behind Bart. "Hi, Chuck. Where are Maeve and Billy?"

"Going to Bart's motor home."

"Wouldn't the guard let you through?"

Chuck started to demur. "I—"

"There were some photographers after Mom!" Bart exploded, then whirled. "Anita, I said she had to be protected, that the media should be clear she was off-limits."

"They've been told," she responded. "Who were they?" she asked Chuck.

"I couldn't see their credentials, but I'd recognize them again. I don't think they'll be bothering her anymore." His jaw clenched. "They got photos, though."

"I'll check into it," Anita promised. "But it wouldn't be the regular NASCAR media. They don't behave like jackals," she said, frowning. "It's not the NASCAR way." Then her expression cleared. "Anyway, Bart—" she nodded toward Chuck "—I think she has protection."

Bart's eyes whipped to his. "What exactly is your interest in my mother?"

"Bartholomew Morgan Branch, where are your manners?"

All three turned to see Maeve at the gate. "Look, Mom, I don't know who this guy is or what he wants from you." His fists were clenched and his gaze was hard as he studied Chuck.

Chuck merely lifted one eyebrow in a clear message that he would not be scared off.

"That is none of your business," Maeve said tartly. "I'm a grown woman."

"But, Mom—"

"Don't 'but, Mom' me, young man." Then she sighed. "Come with me, sweetheart. I'll fix you something to eat while you shower."

"Mom, this is serious."

She tucked her arm into his and tugged. "Poor manners always are. Now come soak your head and wash away your filthy temper." Maeve glanced back at Chuck. "I…" She lifted her shoulders.

"You go on. You have my cell number. Call me when you're ready to go. My plane's here, and I'll take you back to Dallas whenever you're ready."

She hesitated, and he wondered if they were back to square one. Finally she nodded. "All right. Thank you. I'll tell Gideon I don't need his jet."

"I think you should come home with me, Mom," Bart said. "Stay in Charlotte awhile."

Maeve looked torn, and Chuck waited patiently to see what she'd choose.

Then she shook her head. "No, sweetheart, but thank you. You know me—I like to be home in my own bed."

Bart approached Chuck. "My brothers and I will be watching you," he said out of her hearing.

"Understood," Chuck responded without giving an inch.

After a long glare, Bart returned to Maeve's side.

Maeve spoke to Anita. "I need to see Will, too, but…" Left unspoken was her reluctance to go near the media.

Anita nodded. "Don't you worry. We'll go by the media center right now. I'll tell him where you are."

"Thank you." She turned back to Bart, who cast one last warning glare at Chuck before escorting her to his motor home.

"I wanted to talk to Bart," Billy whined after they left.

Anita smiled. "We'll see him at the shop next week, kiddo. Right now, let's find out if Mr. Lawrence would like to have dinner with us."

"But Maeve might…" *need me,* Chuck started to say.

"She's safe inside this lot, and when she calls, we'll get you right back here." Anita sobered. "I'm sorry about those photographers. What did you say to them?"

"Nothing special."

"Somehow I doubt that." She tucked her hand in his elbow while holding Billy's hand with her other. "I'm so glad to see Maeve back, and I wonder if you might not have had a hand in getting her here."

"Maeve's a brave woman all on her own."

"She is," Anita agreed. "And special to all of us." Then she grinned. "But I'm glad she has you on her side, too."

"She's not as sure of that," he said. "But she's been through too much. I'd like to get my hands on that piece of garbage who calls himself her husband."

"Join the club," said Anita.

NEARLY THREE HOURS later, exhausted and heartsore, Maeve rode beside Chuck in a shuttle he'd somehow conjured up. She'd unexpectedly served as the rallying point for her sons to forget their respective finishes and worries over how they'd do in the Chase for the NASCAR Sprint Cup.

Instead, they were united in their disapproval of Chuck. *Who is this guy? We know nothing about him. Don't see him again until we check him out.*

As if their roles were reversed and they were the parents and she the child. She'd barely dissuaded them from calling Penny and Sawyer on the spot, though she felt certain they were on the phone now.

She let her head roll back against the seat cushion and heaved a sigh.

"Did you eat?" Chuck asked.

She looked over at him. "I cooked enough for a small army. As long as I kept their mouths stuffed, they couldn't harangue me."

"About me?"

She nodded. "You'd think I was a teenager going out on her first date." Abruptly she wished she hadn't used that word.

"This wasn't a date." His eyes gleamed even in the darkness. "When we have a date, you'll know it, Maeve."

His voice was a low caress that tugged at something deep in her belly. "I'm not divorced yet."

He took her hand. Brought it to his lips.

Made her shiver.

"You're close enough." When she would have protested, he touched one finger to her lips. "But I'm a patient man where you're concerned." The skin around his eyes crinkled. "Surprises the hell out of me. I didn't make my fortune by being patient." He bent his head to hers, and she forgot how to breathe. "But you're worth waiting for." He brushed his lips over hers.

"I—" All her thoughts scrambled. She could still recall the feeling of having him stand between her and trouble tonight, shielding her as he had at La Mireille. He was a strong, confident man, but he'd also shown gentleness. It would be easy, so very easy to lean toward him and...

She forced herself to sit up. Removed her hand from his. "I'm not ready," she managed, but her voice was still hoarse. Breathy.

His grin was wry. "I'm all too aware of that." He patted her hand once, then faced the front. "That's where the patience comes in."

"I might not ever be," she confessed. "You shouldn't wait for me."

His gaze hardened. "What I choose to do with my time is my decision." Then he looked ahead. "Here we are."

Maeve grasped her purse and let the driver help her out, then he retrieved her suitcase. She followed Chuck to his plane, admiring the lines of it, understanding from her experience with other aircraft that his was topnotch. The interior was understated, no need for the extravagance that Hilton had chosen or the gleaming toys her sons had stocked theirs with.

This plane, like the man, was solid and strong and sure.

But she couldn't afford to get involved with a man like that. She needed to be that way herself. She was through being coddled, kept blind like a hawk being brought to hand by its owner, however much being on her own frightened her.

Were her boys right? Was she too old to find her own way? Had she been caged too long to fly free?

Her mind was spinning with questions and doubts, and a headache was brewing behind her eyes.

"Relax, Maeve. I'm not going to jump you just because I have you at my mercy."

She looked up as he stood over her. "I wasn't thinking any such thing."

He crouched beside her. "You're worrying about something, and you never answered me about whether you'd had dinner."

"I'm not hungry."

He summoned the attendant she hadn't noticed before. "A cup of tea, Earl Grey, I think, and some of those scones. I developed a taste for them when I visited Scotland." At her soft protest, he speared her with a glare. "If you want me to leave you alone, then prove to me you can at least take care of your health."

Her brows snapped together. "I'm not helpless."

"I never said you were. If you'll recall, I said you are one very brave woman." He leaned closer. "But ignoring your physical well-being is dumb, and you're not a dumb woman. Here." He took the tray the attendant held. "Thank you, Lisa." He turned to Maeve. "So if you want to be treated like a grown-up, act like one." He set the tray in her lap, then retreated to the other side of the cabin.

She resisted the urge to toss the whole thing at his head. "You are insufferable, you know that?" She lifted a flaky scone. "Okay, watch." She took a bite, then realized how hungry she was. She hadn't eaten since breakfast.

He did watch her, too closely by half. She would worry about being the prey of this very masculine creature, but she was too intent on devouring every morsel. She cleaned the plate and drained her cup, then rose and approached him. "Satisfied?"

His intense regard nearly burned her up. "Not even close."

Maeve closed her eyes. Touched one hand to her stomach, now filled with butterflies. "Stop that." She turned and walked toward the galley.

The sound of his low chuckle trailed behind her.

It was going to be a long trip back to Dallas.

CHAPTER TEN

A PACKAGE ARRIVED for Maeve the next morning by courier.

To her surprise, she'd slept well last night, even after the events of the previous day, none more challenging than dealing with Chuck Lawrence.

Of course, she'd already had to get through a call from her daughter, Penny, even one from Sawyer, usually the most live-and-let-live of her children. She'd told them crisply that (a) Chuck was just a friend and (b) she was a grown woman.

Neither had been satisfied with that, she thought. But she'd countered by talking with Penny about how the adoption was going and making a date to go baby shopping, and with Sawyer about when he would bring his girlfriend, Lucy, to see her again. Sawyer was somewhat closemouthed, but a willingness to commit was in his gene pool. She'd still bet there was a wedding in the offing and resolved to call Lucy herself.

At last, she had a chance to breathe. She resisted the temptation to call the twins and chew them both out for alarming the others. They loved her, she knew, and felt responsible for her.

That, too, was going to change. She was not an old lady yet, and, God willing, she had a lot of years before she was. She was starting to feel her oats, and she admitted to herself, if not to anyone else, that Chuck Lawrence had a hand in that.

Those eyes, so hot on her. The strong, long-fingered, wide-palmed hands she could almost feel against her skin.

Maeve fanned herself and grinned. "Okay, what's in this package?" she muttered.

"What I want to know is what's going on that's got your cheeks all rosy?" Gerty said from the doorway.

"I didn't hear you come in."

"That's because I had to unload my howitzer. Darn thing's too big for the trunk."

Maeve rolled her eyes and chuckled. "Don't tell me—the boys called you, too."

"They did, then Penny, then Sawyer."

"Good grief. What did you say to them?"

Gerty's eyes twinkled. "That I'd let them know when the wedding was scheduled."

"Gerty! There's not going to be… We're not…" Maeve spluttered.

Gerty laughed. "Gotcha." Then she sobered. "I told them that I like him. That he's a good man. That if you had a lick of sense, you'd start being nicer to him."

"Gerty…" Maeve warned.

"Okay, so I didn't say that last part. But it's true."

Maeve gathered herself to argue, but Gerty stopped her. "When are you going to open his box?"

"How do you know it's from him?"

Gerty simply shrugged.

"Has he talked to you, too?" Maeve set the box down. "Gerty, whose side are you on?"

"Yours, missy. Don't you ever doubt it." She nodded at the package. "Now are you opening it or do *I* have to?"

Maeve fought the temptation to walk away. Or to take it somewhere private to open it. "I need scissors," she said with a huff, and stalked past Gerty into the kitchen. She got the scissors, but found her hands were shaking, and she was clumsy with the tape.

At last, she got the package open.

Inside lay an envelope with her name, nestled on top of the most unique shirt she'd ever seen. The front was emblazoned with the No. 475—Bart's car number—and the back with No. 467, Will's car number. She raised her eyebrows, then opened the envelope. Two tickets spilled out, seats in the grandstands for the Charlotte race, and a note.

You promised you'd teach me, and where better than at the track? The chopper pilot said you couldn't really experience a race from a suite, so I got us seats in the stands. We'll just go as normal fans. I'll pick you up at noon on Thursday.

Chuck

P.S.: I hope you like your shirt. I have one just like it, only opposite sides. The boys can't say we're not trying to be fair.

She burst out laughing.

Then she got peeved. "That man!" she fumed, pacing the kitchen. "I didn't say I'd go with him to a race. Who does he think he is?"

"You ever stop to think how much trouble he went to, getting those shirts made and tickets here overnight?"

"I didn't ask him to do any of this. He's assuming too much."

"Are you or are you not going to the rest of the races?"

Maeve glanced at her friend. "Yes, but—"

"So what does it hurt to be there with him? Save your boys the trouble of figuring out how to get you there and what to do with you when they got plenty on their minds already."

Maeve frowned. "That's a low blow." But Gerty's aim was true—the Chase for the NASCAR Sprint Cup was crucial to the boys' futures, and after all they'd battled through this season, thanks to their father, she didn't like burdening them further.

"What's the harm? The man done anything to you besides be nice."

Nice. Her lips twitched, remembering his reaction to the word.

"Uh-huh," Gerty said. "More than nice, maybe?"

Maeve straightened instantly. "I'm still married. And it's none of your business."

Gerty snorted. "Good for him." Then she walked off, humming.

Maeve glared after her, then looked again at the note, the tickets. The shirt.

What was the harm, indeed? She lifted the shirt and held it against herself, shaking her head.

Chuck Lawrence might be a kind man.

But he was anything but harmless.

She walked up the stairs to try on the shirt.

"CHUCK, DEAR," said the very familiar voice of Cecily Dunstan. "What's this I hear about you and Maeve Branch?"

He was on his way to pick up Maeve, and he wished he hadn't taken this call, though he knew gossip wasn't Cecily's scene. "She's just a friend." Damn. Now he was sounding like Maeve.

"Really? That enraged-bear pose at the race track looked much more like a man protecting something precious."

"Cecily, you know me better than that."

"And *you* know *me* better than to believe I'm buying this line about friendship."

He and Cecily truly were friends—okay, friends with benefits. The relationship served them both well, as neither was interested in a long-term commitment but both enjoyed the other's company.

They generally spoke very frankly to each other, but Chuck found himself unwilling to discuss Maeve with her. "She's had a hard time," was all he said.

"So this is about pity?"

"Maeve is not pitiful. She's a brave woman who's struggling right now and…" He stopped himself.

But not before Cecily heard more than he'd intended. "Oh, dear." She sighed. "I knew this would happen one day."

He frowned. "What do you mean?"

"Chuck, you had a wonderful marriage. I always knew you'd want to be married again one day to the right woman. You're a romantic, my friend."

"What?" he scoffed. "I am no such thing. And Maeve isn't yet divorced, and anyway, she's not ready."

Cecily's laughter trilled. "Don't sound so disgruntled. Where's that patience you always keep saying you've developed?"

"I have plenty of it. It's just…" He raked fingers through his hair.

"That's one way I knew we would never be more than friends, you know." Her tone was fond, if a little sad. "Because you found it easy to be patient with me." She was silent for a minute. "She may not be ready for a long time after what she's been through, you know?"

"There's no rush," he said blithely. *Oh, don't you*

wish, he thought. *Now you're lying to yourself, son.* He'd had one restless night after another since Talladega. He'd filled his days with work and more work, then punishing games of racquetball.

But the woman had gotten under his skin. Damn it.

"Poor Chuck," said Cecily.

"Don't 'poor Chuck' me. I'm fine. Absolutely fine."

Another peal of laughter. "Want to grab dinner and a movie tonight for distraction?"

"I can't." He hesitated. "I'm picking up Maeve now to go to a race this weekend."

"Oh, my. You do have it bad. NASCAR now, is it?"

"It's an interesting sport," he grumbled. "Watch a race, or better yet, go to one. It gets in your blood." Or maybe it was just Maeve who'd gotten into his blood.

"Thanks, darling, but I'll just take you at your word." Then her tone turned serious. "Be careful. I don't want you getting hurt."

"Me?" He was astounded at the notion. "I'm fine, just fine. Maeve's the one who needs help."

"Well, all I can say is I hope the lady understands how lucky she is."

He wasn't at all sure Maeve would put things that way. He'd all but strong-armed her into going with him this weekend. Okay, he *had* strong-armed her.

"Your silence concerns me," Cecily said. "Shall I call and tell her?"

"No!" he said hastily. "Cecily, I can handle this fine by myself."

"I certainly hope so. You just remember that I'm here if you need me. We can still be friends, right?" Her tone sounded wistful, and truth be told, he felt somewhat wistful himself. They'd done well together, even though they'd agreed from the first that neither wanted more.

"Of course we can," he said. "And thanks."

"Goodbye, Chuck." The click of disconnection he'd never thought much about before sounded so final.

"Goodbye, Cecily," he said into an empty phone line.

HE'D BEEN RIGHT to strong-arm her into this.

Maeve was having fun. She looked…cute. Since it was a night race, she wore no hat, needing no shade from the sun, a prime concern for him, given her fair skin, and the only reason he'd chosen seats in the stands.

She stood beside him, clad in her half-Bart, half-Will shirt and jeans with sneakers, headset around her neck, as they waited for the race to begin. They were packed in like sardines, and Chuck's protective instincts were on overdrive, but thus far, their seat-mates were pleasant and eager to exchange race tidbits with her. None seemed to recognize her, and she had relaxed more with every minute that passed. The only special notice she'd garnered was because of her unusual shirt. She'd simply said she couldn't choose between the brothers.

She'd cheered loudly for both of them during introductions, bouncing on her toes and managing an earsplitting whistle more common to teenage boys than the society matron most people knew her to be.

During the national anthem and the flyover, she'd gotten teary-eyed and leaned into him a bit. He'd slipped one arm around her shoulders and resisted the urge to kiss her.

"Put on your headset if you don't like it really loud," she said as the grand marshal was introduced. "You can't imagine the noise when all forty-three engines crank up at the same time."

He shook his head. "I want to hear it first."

She grinned. "I don't blame you. It never fails to give me goose bumps."

"That's what the copter pilot said."

"Just wait, you'll see. And you'll never forget it."

Then the cry went out: "Gentlemen...start your engines!" And Chuck heard it—felt it, really, all the way through his body—that growling, belly-deep roar louder than anything he'd ever heard in his life. He turned to her. "Awesome!" Exactly what his sons would have said in his position. He blinked. "Incredible."

"Wait until they go green. This is nothing." She grinned at him, then pointed to his headset, which was tied into hers so they could speak on the intercom when the race was under way. "You'll be glad of it soon."

"Maybe," he said as the cars rolled down pit road

and onto the track behind the pace car. "But not yet." The pilot had been right—the race at Talladega had been interesting, but here, excitement flowed through the crowd like high-voltage electricity. Everyone was on their feet, the anticipation palpable as the cars circled the track.

She wasn't wrong. The noise level was beyond loud, yet for some reason he wanted to experience the full of it, just once. He watched the pace car peel off onto pit road, then heard the cars ratchet up the speed as the green flag dropped and the crowd screamed and the hair on his skin rose…

Maeve threw herself at him and hugged him. "You've got the fever," she shouted in his ear. "I love it!"

He picked her up and kissed her once, hard. *I love you,* he almost said, and the words were like having cold water dumped over his head—shocking, exhilarating, scary as hell.

Her eyes were wide, her pupils huge and dark, and he couldn't tell which of them was more stunned. The noise level was staggering, yet there was a bubble around them. All he could see was Maeve, all he could hear—

She blinked then and stepped back, and the bubble shattered. She pointed to his headset as she donned her own. Then she faced the track, her face set and still and troubled.

He fumbled for the intercom switch and found it. "It's okay, Maeve. Just enjoy the race."

She turned to him, eyes swimming. "I'm sorry. I just…I got carried away."

"It's not a sin to enjoy yourself, sweetheart."

The endearment made her press her lips together tightly. He wanted to push her to acknowledge what was growing between them, wanted to shake her until she admitted that this was special.

Where's that patience? Cecily had asked.

Where indeed? He closed his eyes, shook his head. *That's one way I knew we would never be more than friends*, she'd said. *Poor Chuck.*

All right. He could do this. Damned if he wouldn't. He glanced down and saw Maeve standing stiffly beside him, all her excitement gone. He bent and nudged her. "Want to wager on which of our guys knocks that insufferable O'Bryan out of first?" He found a grin from somewhere and made it real.

Her smile was slow in coming, but at last she brightened. "I'm supposed to root for Bart today, since he's the underdog."

"Hey, Will hasn't had the chance to feel a need to punch me out yet. Maybe he won't if I put my money on him."

Maeve grinned. "I wouldn't count on it. The phone wires to Penny in Dallas and Sawyer in Raleigh nearly melted after last week."

"What did you tell them?"

"Same thing I told the twins. Mind your own business."

He gave her a thumbs-up. "Attagirl." When she

smiled wider in gratitude and merriment, he knew he had to get his mind off those lips. "So explain to me about this lucky dog rule."

Maeve turned her attention back to the race as she filled him in. When, moments later, Bart charged up the field and closed in on Rafael O'Bryan, she jumped up and down, pumping her fist in the air.

Then she glanced over at him and winked.

Patience, Chuck counseled himself as he pretended to pout. When she laughed, he experienced the reward of his efforts.

KENT GROSSO won this time, after a long series of poor finishes at Charlotte. Dean Grosso came in second, and Bart was third. Will finished fifth, while Justin Murphy came in eighth, and the overbearingly cocky Rafael O'Bryan only managed seventh, dropping him to second in the points after managing to make it to first after Talladega.

Will rose one spot to sixth in the standings, while Bart also climbed one notch to seventh.

"I guess I owe you on our bet," Maeve said to Chuck as they lingered in the stands as the crowd was filing out. Will had passed O'Bryan first. "Except we didn't set an amount."

"No," he said, his eyes glowing, "we didn't. Got any ideas?"

She dug in the pocket of her jeans. "I'm not sure how much I have with me."

"You could use your imagination," he said, his tone low and caressing.

Her heart did a little flip. "Like maybe I buy you an ice cream?" she teased, but her voice wobbled a little.

His steady regard warmed her. Made her nervous. She kept remembering the feel of him, so strong, so lean and hard as he lifted her to him. Kissed her. What she wouldn't do for another embrace!

If only she dared. "Maybe cook you dinner?"

She saw that he was remembering, too, and she steeled herself for him to suggest something more intimate.

But he surprised her with a nod. "Great idea. When?"

She was half-relieved, half-disappointed. Completely confused. "Um…Monday? Tuesday?"

"Why not both?"

Her eyes widened. "Um—"

He laughed. "Okay, Tuesday. *And* you let me go to Martinsville with you." When she opened her mouth to protest, he continued. "I'm going, anyway, with you or without you. I'm completely hooked." He grasped her elbow before she could respond. "So both boys get to be in the media center, right? So neither should be *vexed?*"

His wide grin was irresistible. She chuckled. "Oh, they can always find something to compete over. If they'd tied for first, they'd be comparing pit-stop times."

"So do you need to cook for them or can we take them out to dinner, my treat?"

"Aren't you the brave one?"

He shrugged. "Avoiding things doesn't make them vanish. My way is to face obstacles head-on."

She resisted pointing out that her way was more the avoidance route—or had been. "What if I'm not ready for that?"

She could see his disappointment, but his tone was not disparaging. "I can go on to dinner, and you can call when you're ready for me to pick you up, just like last time."

It was tempting. Doing so would definitely be easier.

Sure, Maeve, run again. Hide, as you've been doing.

She took a deep breath, then grasped his arm. "In for a penny, in for a pound. Let's go beard the lions in their dens."

"Were you an English major?" he asked, grinning.

She burst into delighted laughter. "Okay, okay, mixed metaphors—but you get the point."

He tucked her hand into his elbow, gazing down at her with something that seemed to be affection and pride. "I do, Maeve. I surely do." He led her up the stands behind the thinning crowd.

CHAPTER ELEVEN

ON TUESDAY NIGHT, MAEVE HEARD the doorbell ring and placed one hand to her chest in an unconscious effort to slow her racing heart. She'd come so close to begging Gerty to stay for this meal with Chuck, unnerved by what he might expect from her, what the meal might mean, how she would handle—

A second chime sounded. She smoothed her hair, closed her eyes for a second and took a deep breath, then crossed through the dining room and living room to the entry where she could see him framed in the beveled glass of her front door.

She'd survived a meal with Chuck and her twins, however grudgingly the boys had accepted his presence. She could do this. With shaking fingers, she clasped the handle and opened the door. "Hi."

He produced another bouquet, this time a dainty one of violets and alyssum. "Hi. You look amazing."

She glanced down at the filmy, flowing lavender skirt and short-sleeved sweater she'd chosen as much because they soothed her as for how they looked. She'd only gone through about eight outfits this time before deciding. "Thank you." She took the bouquet. "These are lovely." She paused. "And you look very nice yourself."

He looked more than nice. He wore the Texas equivalent of dress clothes—a white, long-sleeved shirt and jeans with a razor-sharp crease atop well-worn cowboy boots. Hilton had disdained the look as too blue collar, the response of a man who'd done everything possible to bury his past, to pretend he was to the manor born.

Maeve's experience thus far with Chuck led her to believe that however far he'd climbed from his beginnings, he'd never forsaken them. He'd embraced his roots.

She'd grown up in the polo shirt–khaki crowd, but she'd always had a weakness for the look Chuck wore with the confidence of someone who has nothing to prove.

In a word, he looked hot. Very hot. He might be in his mid-fifties, but that only added to his appeal. Pretty-boy male models had no character in their faces. Chuck Lawrence, she was afraid, had both character and sex appeal—and the air of a man who knew his way around a bedroom.

However little intention she had of baring hers. The very thought terrified her.

He misinterpreted her expression. "I promise my boots are clean, even though I was with my horses this afternoon."

"I wasn't worried."

"Then may I come in?"

"Oh!" She stepped aside. "I'm sorry. I don't know what I was thinking."

"Maybe something like I was thinking about you?" His grin was pure mischief.

She was not going there. She grasped for a switch in direction. "You have horses?"

His look told her he knew exactly what she was doing. "I do. On a little place near Waxahachie. Do you ride?"

She led the way back to the kitchen to put the flowers in water. "I used to, when I was younger."

"Why did you stop? Did you like it?"

"I absolutely adored it. My favorite horse was named Luke, a palomino."

"I tend toward paints myself, but palominos are sure good-looking. Bet you made a picture on the back of one. Why did you stop?" he repeated.

"Oh, you know, children, all of that." She waved it off as though it hadn't torn her heart out when Hilton had pressured her to either sell her horse or take up dressage or steeplechase because they were more impressive.

"I'd love to take you riding. I have a terrific mare that might suit you."

"Because she's gentle?"

He arched an eyebrow. "No, because she's spirited. She needs someone with a little fire to ride her."

He was standing close, very close. The scent of

him, something woodsy and utterly male, slipped past the floral fragrance and curled down inside her.

She scrambled to remember what he'd said. "You think I have fire? No one else does."

"There's a lot smoldering inside this ladylike package, Miss Maeve." His eyes echoed the heat. "I'm thinking you'd enjoy someone fanning it into flame."

The shock of it, the delicious threat, sent a shudder right down her spine. She whirled away. "Would you care for some wine?" She focused on the bottles she'd set out, the corkscrew that suddenly seemed impossible to operate.

"Here, let me." He reached right over her shoulder, bringing his chest into contact with her back.

Maeve went rigid, trapped between his big, hard body and the counter. She couldn't catch her breath, even as something inside her softened, readied itself for him. Like a stallion covering a mare, he was danger. He was excitement. Unbearable thrill.

At last he stepped away and began uncorking the wine.

Maeve drew an unsteady breath. Clenched her fingers on the counter's edge and concentrated on slowing her heart.

"I hope you like salmon," she said, forcing herself to turn.

He poured each of them a glass and handed hers over, his warm fingers brushing hers. "I'm not hard to please." His eyes locked on hers. "I make it a habit to enjoy a lot of things. To be open to experimenting."

Maeve gulped hard at the implied promise. Took a sip of her wine, then crossed to the refrigerator, taking out a salad.

Cursed herself for being so foolhardy as to set them a table in the conservatory, a far too romantic setting for the danger Chuck represented.

But correcting that now would only clue him in as to how nervous he made her. "Would you bring the wine, please?"

"I'll do most anything you ask, darlin'."

She whirled. "Stop that."

He grinned. "Stop what?"

"That...that flirting. I'm not... You can't—"

"I said 'most anything,' sweet Maeve. But I'm afraid that's not included. I promised I'd be patient, and though I don't like it, I will. But if you ask me to stop making you feel like the beautiful woman you are, I'm afraid that's where I just can't oblige you." He smiled. "What's the harm in it?"

"I'm not beautiful," she said. "I'm getting old. I have..." Past caution now, she confessed to the worst of it. "I have wrinkles. My skin sags in places it didn't before."

He threw his head back and laughed. "You think that's going to scare me away? Those lines are battle scars, and hell, I don't look like I used to, either." His expression grew serious. "We've lived, Maeve, and we've got the medals to prove it. We're not those images in magazines, models barely past childhood."

"But..." He'd laughed at what shamed her. Oddly enough, admitting it didn't hurt as she'd expected it to.

"But, but, but." He set the bottle down on the table and took the salad bowl from her hands. "You are the most contrary woman I have ever met, I swear, but you know what? I am the master of scaling obstacles. Been doing it all my life, when the prize is worth it." He pulled back her chair. "Now here we are in this breathtaking space where there are all sorts of plants I don't know the names of." He scooted her in and rounded the table to his own seat, gripping the back. "I've got you all flustered. It's fun for me and good for you, if you'd admit it. But you're not ready to, so we're going to drop the topic for now about how I am going to get you in bed someday and you are very much going to enjoy it." He lowered himself into his own chair. "So—" he gestured around them, then pointed to a plant off to his left "—tell me the name of that one first."

Maeve stared at him, frowning slightly. Confused and relieved and...hopeful. He'd said *someday,* and even though she was a million miles from ready for the getting-in-bed part, he gave her a reason to believe that everything in her life wasn't crumbling, that someday—*someday,* a potent and cheerful word—good things would happen. That she had a new reason to keep trying to climb out of this disaster her life had become.

"I don't understand you," she said.

"That's okay, darlin'. I don't understand you, either, not completely." He grinned. "But we'll make it up as we go. Let's just have some fun and see if the riddles solve themselves while we're at it." He grasped for the salad tongs. "Hand me your plate, Maeve, and start naming plants."

She felt the press of tears, but not sad ones, for a change. These tears were sheer gratitude.

"That's a *Ficus benjamina,* and persnickety as a plant gets."

"It looks happy in here," he said, and glanced around. "And I can't blame it. You look happy here, too."

She smiled and picked up her fork. "It's my favorite room in the house."

"It's like you," he said, his eyes warm. "A lovely place at the end of a stormy, dark road."

She swallowed hard as her heart turned over and a single tear fell. "Thank you."

"No need to say thanks for the truth," he said gently. Then he pulled his gaze away, and she couldn't decide whether to be sad or relieved because of all his look seemed to contain. "So…what's that one?"

She followed the direction he was pointing.

And went on with the naming.

"THAT WAS AMAZING. I have an excellent cook available when I need him, but I'm ready to fire him after this. You need a job?"

Maeve smiled. "I might. I hadn't really thought about cooking for a living. I don't really have any job skills to speak of."

"Are you serious? I can think of half a dozen business ideas right offhand for which you'd be perfect."

She looked skeptical. "Like what?"

"Maeve, you could run a bed-and-breakfast, you could open your own restaurant." He waved at the plants around them. "You have a green thumb quite obviously, so how about a nursery or a landscape-design firm? The house itself is an impressive mix of stunning and warm, so unless someone else decorated it…"

"No. Just me."

"There you go. Interior design—another option." He ticked them off on his fingers.

"I never even considered owning my own business." She appeared lost in thought. "Anyway, I don't have the money to start one unless I sell my house, and I don't think I can until the courts are done with Hilton. From what I gathered from my former lawyers, homestead law protects it except from a mortgage lender—which, thank heavens, there's not—but not from the IRS, so I could still be in trouble. For now, though, as long as I can pay the property taxes, I can stay, but there's the rub. This place is expensive to maintain."

He wanted to make a lot of promises about her future, but she was not remotely ready to hear them—and every once in a while, he got a little nervous himself that he was actually considering something permanent, a move he'd foresworn after his wife died.

But there was one promise he could make. "I'd invest in you."

That brought a full-fledged frown. "No. That's not an option."

"Why not? I invest in promising entrepreneurs all the time."

"This is different. We're…" She halted.

He kept the lid on the smile rising inside him. "We're what?"

She waved it off. "I don't know, and I'm not talking about it. You make me nervous."

This time the smile wouldn't be denied. "So we keep dancing around the topic of when I take you to bed and how very much you're going to enjoy it?"

She cast him a quelling glance, but he could see the faint curve to her lips. "We do."

He sighed. "You're a harsh taskmistress." He rose and grabbed both their plates. "You cooked. I'll do the dishes." He hadn't been married for twenty-six years without understanding some of the things that really appealed to a woman.

"You don't have to. You're my guest."

"Yeah, but this way I get to stay longer, and I impress you, in the bargain." He grinned.

She smiled and shook her head. "You are incorrigible."

"Oh, darlin', how you flatter."

They laughed together, and the moment was rich and delicious.

As they strolled toward the kitchen, he decided to press his luck. No guts, no glory. "So since we'll be at Martinsville next weekend, I have a suggestion."

She set down the wine bottle and glasses. "Did I agree to go to Martinsville with you?"

He clutched his heart. "You are surely not going to tell me you're reneging on a wager that you, I might add, lost? I thought better of you." He sighed dramatically.

"We'll leave aside the matter of whether I actually agreed to a two-part payoff—this dinner and Martinsville. Or you just did another of your land grabs and assumed—"

"You wound me, sweetheart. I've never grabbed land in my life. Well, not without paying for it."

"As little as possible would be my guess."

But her eyes were twinkling. "The art of the deal, ma'am. Anyway, about my suggestion—"

"I'm afraid to hear."

"Buck up, Miss Maeve. You can handle it." He turned to the sink and began running water. She might not believe it, but he was nervous. "There's this mountain place I know about in Asheville that's a perfect vacation spot. Asheville's just a hop over from Martinsville, and I think you need some R & R.

What say we don't come back to Dallas before the Atlanta race but, instead, stay on the East Coast for the week? Ever been to Asheville?"

She shook her head. "I hear it's beautiful."

"You'd go nuts over the gardens at Biltmore, the Vanderbilt estate. This place isn't far away."

"What kind of place?" She was frowning again. Worrying. "I'd have to pay my own way."

What she didn't have to say was that she couldn't afford it. "That's the best part—it belongs to someone I know." She didn't need to hear that the someone was himself. He pressed his advantage before she could come up with more objections. "It's nothing fancy, but the view can't be beat. Wouldn't you like a chance to get away from Dallas and NASCAR and all the attention and just…chill?"

Temptation danced in her eyes, but caution remained. "This wouldn't have to do with that bed scenario, would it?"

In this, at least, he could be totally honest. "Babe, you just say the word—" she was already shutting down, backing up "—but if you don't, it's hands-off." He held up a hand. "Scout's honor."

"I bet you weren't even a Scout."

"I read the handbook once—does that count?" When she didn't smile, he sobered, too. "Honest to God, Maeve. I'm clear on what I want, but I have never forced a woman in my life, and I never will. I just want you to have a break, I swear. You need one, and there's nothing better than mountain air for relaxing. I don't care if you sleep the whole week away."

She studied him. "I don't know what to do. I don't like it that you're using your plane and you're buying tickets and dinners."

"Sweetheart, I have more money than I'll ever spend, and my kids are taken care of already. It's not charity, I swear." He waggled his eyebrows, hoping to lighten the mood. "I haff ulterior motiffs." He twirled an imaginary mustache.

"That's what I'm afraid of. I'm not ready, Chuck. I might never be."

He clasped her shoulders and drew her near. She resisted at first, but then laid her head against his chest, and he vowed to battle the devil himself to make her life better.

Even if he had to battle her own doubts first. "It's okay, Maeve," he murmured as he closed his arms around her and rocked her gently side to side. "I told you I make a good friend. Regardless of anything else, I don't take that offer lightly. Let me be your friend and give you a place to heal for a while, will you?"

She didn't answer at first, and he got lost in the feel of her, experiencing something deeper and more tender than desire.

At last her head rose. "I'll do all the cooking. It's the least I can contribute."

"Not that I would ever turn down your cooking, sweetheart, but that's a deal-breaker. I grill a mean steak, and I'm not half-bad at breakfast." As she gathered herself to protest, he reminded himself that her pride had been battered enough the past several months. "How about we go fifty-fifty? Whoever doesn't cook cleans up?"

She stared into his eyes as if searching for how much she could trust him. He felt a twinge of guilt that he hadn't been honest about his ownership of the cabin, but she needed this too much, and he was afraid that bit of information would keep her from accepting.

She backed away, and for a minute he thought he'd overplayed his hand, probably because he'd broken a cardinal rule of his own and cared too much about the outcome. You make mistakes in business if you get too personally invested.

But this wasn't business, and he was rusty at love.

"Gerty would take care of Harry for me, I guess." Her hand rose from her side, and she extended it to shake. "All right, deal." She smiled, but the smile was not her bright, excited one, and he regretted pushing her into what he believed best for her.

Well, a little, at least. The fact remained that she needed the break, and she'd never take one on her own.

"Thanks," he said, and clasped her hand. Barely resisted pulling her to him, but the fine balance could be destroyed too easily. He'd retire from the field and live to battle another day.

"It's you who deserves thanks," she said. "Even if I'm not exactly sure how I got outmaneuvered."

"I promise you'll like it. Does that help?"

"Does anyone ever say no to you? I'm just curious."

"Not too often."

"I'm going to practice," she said. The teasing twinkle returned, though he wasn't at all sure she wasn't serious.

"Oh, honey, there are so many better ways for you to spend your time."

She laughed and flicked a handful of soap bubbles at him.

Then squealed as he returned the favor. And gave back as good as she got.

What a woman.

CHAPTER TWELVE

"I HAVE NO BUSINESS doing this," Maeve muttered to Harry as she packed. Harry only groaned and rolled over. "It's just not sensible. Not…seemly." And didn't that sound exactly like words that could have come out of her very proper mother's mouth?

"Who are you talking to?" Gerty asked as she entered.

"The dog. Or Chuck. Maybe the air. I don't know." Anguished, she faced her friend. "This is a bad idea, isn't it?"

"A getaway with a good-looking man who cares about you?" Gerty clucked her tongue. "Did somebody drop you on your head when you were young? If you don't want to go, I will."

"No. I…" Maeve's protest died. "I mean, you probably should, but I…I want to, it's just that—"

"If you say to me one more time that you're still married, I'm going to scream. The divorce will be final any day, and Hilton has never honored his vows, anyway, so why—"

"Should I?" Maeve asked. "Because I'm not like

Hilton." She resumed packing. "Anyway, nothing's going to happen. Chuck and I are just friends."

"Uh-huh." Gerty's tone was unconvinced.

Maeve was about to protest when the phone rang. She moved to her bedside and picked it up. "Hello?"

"Mrs. Branch, my name is Howard Sampson. Chuck Lawrence asked me to call you."

"Why?"

"I'm a financial manager. I've studied your situation so that I can help you straighten out your finances."

Maeve's eyebrows rose nearly to her hairline. "Oh, you have, have you?"

"Mr. Lawrence wanted me to have some suggestions ready for you as quickly as possible. I was happy to invest the time in advance to make our time together more efficient."

"More efficient." Maeve glanced at Gerty and frowned. "What sort of time commitment did you envision?"

"Whatever it takes, Mrs. Branch. Mr. Lawrence wants you to have good advice. I'm proud to say he considers me top tier. I have long-time clientele, any of whom would be glad to give you references, if Mr. Lawrence's recommendation doesn't suffice."

Her head was spinning. "How did you obtain the information to study my…situation?"

"Mr. Lawrence had already assembled a very complete file. I only had to augment it a little."

"I see." Now it was Gerty who was frowning.

Maeve simply shook her head. "And what are your rates, Mr. Hampson?"

"My rates are not a concern. That is, they'll be quite reasonable."

A picture was forming, and Maeve's vision was going red around the edges. She started yanking items out of her suitcase and tossing them aside. "Would that happen to be because Mr. Lawrence would be paying you, as well? Or did he perhaps intend for you not to bill me at all?"

"Um, well...you see, Mrs. Branch—"

"Oh, I see just fine. Thank you for your call, Mr. Sampson. Your services won't be needed."

"But—"

"Have a nice day now." Maeve slammed down the phone. Kicked the bedside table and yelped at the pain. "That jerk! The unmitigated gall of him!" She stamped around her room, limping slightly. Harry was on his feet, too, now. "How could he? Have I ever asked for his charity? Did I not make myself clear that I have to handle this on my own? How dare he!" She charged back to her suitcase and began emptying it. "I'm not going, that's all. I'm just not." She sank to the mattress. Harry nudged her hand with his head. She petted him absently. "But I promised the boys. I have to make the race." She looked up at Gerty. "I don't know how to book airfares online. Do you?"

"Slow down now," Gerty responded. "Talk to me before you do something stupid. Best I can figure from your side of the conversation, Chuck tried to help you with something that's got you hopping mad. What was it?"

"That—" she pointed at the telephone "—that man is a financial manager. Chuck—" the emphasis on his name was not a kind one "—ever so helpfully sent him my way, after first providing him with a complete file on my finances so that he could efficiently—" the word came out a growl "—make the best use of our time together as he advised me on how to make it through the tangle Hilton left me in."

Gerty blew out a breath. "O-kay. So Chuck meant well."

"Meant well?" Maeve held back a scream. "He dug into my finances—God knows how, but I've lived with Hilton long enough to know money can buy most anything." She began to pace. "But that wasn't enough. Oh, no, he's subsidizing that man's fees because poor little Maeve is too broke. Mr. Sampson was probably going to charge me a pittance, just to soothe my pride, while the big, strong man took care of the little woman." She slapped her open palm against the wall. "Well, I won't have it, I tell you. I've been the little woman for thirty-odd years, and where did it get me? Broke and disgraced and—" her voice wobbled "—a fool." She swiped angrily at her eyes. "A pathetic fool."

The phone rang and Maeve glared at it. Refused to answer.

"It might be your children," Gerty muttered, and

passed in front of her to snatch up the receiver. "Hello?" She listened for a second, her eyes cutting toward Maeve.

"Forget it," Maeve said. "If that's Chuck, I'm not speaking to him. Just tell him that Asheville's off, and I'll be making my own arrangements for Martinsville."

Gerty started to speak, but Maeve could hear Chuck's urgent tone, if not his words. She listened for a moment, glanced at Maeve again, but her expression was unreadable. "Huh. Well, good luck with that." She hung up.

"What did he say?"

Gerty crossed the room. "Why do you care? You want to find out, talk to him yourself." She turned and left.

Maeve was flabbergasted. She started to follow Gerty, then changed her mind. Still fuming, she carried some of the clothes she'd planned to take to the mountains back to her chest of drawers. She didn't care. Whatever he had to say, it made no difference to her. The bottom line was that he'd interfered, had taken control, not trusting her to manage her own life. He'd breached her privacy, to boot, and that thought only fanned the flames of her anger.

How dare he? He didn't understand her at all. Wasn't she trying her best to pick up the pieces and bring order to her life? Maybe she didn't know all she should yet, but she didn't need to be cosseted or patted on the head like a good little girl and told to go wait in the corner while some man made all the decisions for her.

She slapped down the stack of folded clothes and marched to the phone, ready to give Chuck Lawrence a piece of her mind. She snatched up the receiver, then put it down. No. No, she would not deign to speak to him, there was no reason. They weren't suited, and she was surely out of her mind for ever softening toward him. She was done with men for the foreseeable future, end of story. She nearly tripped over Harry as she stalked around the room.

"Oh, I'm sorry, sweetheart. I didn't hurt you, did I?" She would focus on her children, on Harry. On the animals in the shelter. And she would study as hard as she needed to sort out her situation.

She plopped to the floor beside the old dog, who leaned into her with a groan of contentment. All the steam ran out of her then. She bent her head to his, drained by the uproar. "Just you and me, Harry," she murmured.

She had no idea how long she'd been there when she heard footfalls pound up the stairs. She sat up straight just as a large frame filled the doorway.

"Go away." She focused on Harry, scratching behind his ears. He crawled onto her lap. "I have nothing to say to you."

Chuck merely leaned against the door frame, the picture of indolence. "Suit yourself." Arms crossed over his chest, he acted as if he had all the time in the world.

Maeve didn't know what to do.

Then she found herself spoiling for a fight. Harry, sensing the tension, rose and headed for the kitchen. Maeve pushed to her feet and stalked toward Chuck. "You have a lot of nerve." She poked him in the chest.

He gripped her hand, and that was when she got a good look at him.

And realized that his eyes were not nearly so complacent as his pose.

She tried to yank her hand away, but he wouldn't let go. "Unhand me."

"So we're back to that, are we, *Princess?*" The emphasis was not complimentary. "Dismiss the peon out of hand? I try to help you, and this is the thanks I get?"

She used her other hand to push against him. "Help me? You spied on me. Gave private information to a stranger! How could you?"

"I shared nothing that's not public knowledge, Maeve. Like it or not, your life has been an open book the past several months. I'm not the vulture who exposed you. You can thank your husband for that." He switched his grasp on her hand to a caress. "You can talk to Howard or not. Share with him whatever you'd like should you choose to use him. He's good, Maeve, very good. I honestly wanted to help you, but I could tell you didn't feel comfortable talking to me about specifics." He bent closer. "I'm worried about you. I don't want to see you hurt anymore."

She believed the sincerity she saw, but still… "What about his fees? He implied you were taking care of them. I'm not a charity case."

He rolled his eyes. "Howard is great with numbers, a genius, in fact, but he's lousy with words—and people. What he should have said is that he works for me. I knew you were worried about money—you told me your last firm abandoned you because there was nothing in it for them." He interlaced their fingers. "Howard is such a whiz kid that I can't always keep him busy. I thought he could help you out, and he's someone who already has a nice income, so he doesn't need to gouge you. I understood that your pride wouldn't let you use him for free, so I suggested he should charge you something because I know you don't want charity." He lifted his shoulders. "Maybe I'm no better with words than Howard, but all I can say is that I meant well."

Her fury had dimmed, but she still had to be sure he understood.

"I won't apologize for wanting to help you," he said. "But I will say I'm sorry if I handled it wrong. Please don't turn away help simply out of pride."

"I won't be pitied."

"I feel many things for you, Maeve—some I don't understand myself, and I can't say I like it—but pity is not one of them." He stepped back. "And I also hope you won't rob yourself of a chance to recharge by refusing to go to Asheville."

"You keep pushing me."

"Then push back, damn it. I won't break—and I won't betray you, either, just because we disagree."

"I still can't go."

She could see his own temper stirring. "Is that how you are? I make one mistake, and that's it? No second chances, no forgiveness?"

Maeve was shocked. "I'm not… I don't…" She halted. Stared at nothing as she tried to process this novel thought. Then she faced him. "No. I'm not like that. I just…" She rubbed her forehead. "I'm so confused." So tired of trying to adapt to a world gone topsy-turvy.

"Let's reduce it to the simplest terms, then. I'm going to Martinsville; you're going to Martinsville. I have a plane; it's making the trip, anyway. Bring what you need for Asheville. No commitment. If you decide to come back home instead, that's fine. I have plenty of work to be done here, and we'll just return after the race. Take it one day at a time, Maeve. See how you feel by Sunday. Just don't cheat yourself trying to spite me."

She stared at him. Hilton would never in a million years have been so understanding. She found it hard to trust that Chuck really meant this, but his expression seemed sincere. "How can I be worth this much trouble?"

His gaze was sorrowful. "What I want to know is what that son of a bitch did to convince you that you're not." He took her hand again, lifted it to his lips. "Let's just go root for your boys, Maeve, and let everything else be for now. Fair enough?"

The soft press of his lips nearly undid her. Inside her, something relaxed. "I guess."

"That's my girl." He smiled. "Pick you up at two."

She waved goodbye and escorted him down to the entry.

When he was gone, she cast an alarmed glance at the clock.

And raced back up the stairs.

CHAPTER THIRTEEN

"WHAT GOOD will it do you to go to Charlotte instead of Asheville?" Gerty asked when Maeve called her from Martinsville.

"Will bruised his hand, slamming it into the wall of the garage. Bart is happy, yes, having moved up a notch in the points thanks to a third-place finish, but Will is beside himself after two bad pit stops in a row knocked him back to fourteenth. He dropped two spots in the Chase, Gerty—two. There are only four races to go."

"Does he or does he not have a girlfriend, Maeve? She can tend his wounds. Face it, he won't want his mother hovering over him. You know how he is. He just has to brood for a day or so, then he'll be fighting mad and ready to race again."

"But..." Maeve sighed. "He goes through girl-friends like water. Both of them do."

"They're grown men. They don't need their mommy."

Maeve winced. "I wouldn't—"

"You would. Not that your boys don't adore you, because they do. But the best thing you can do for them is show them that you're getting your own life back. Quite honestly, Maeve, they've got enough on their minds without worrying about you."

"So I just go shack up with the first attractive man who asks me out? That's really going to make them happy."

"You'll seize any excuse, won't you?" Gerty said. "Tell me this—have you enjoyed the trip with Chuck so far? Has he lived up to his word and let you take each day as it comes? Now don't you try lying to me. I know you too well."

"I guess."

"You sound like a rebellious teenager."

"If only I were that young."

Gerty snorted. "Don't be an idiot, Maeve. Go to Asheville." Her tone gentled. "He's not some pimpled boy. He's a man of his word. Just go to the mountains and relax. Take it as it comes." Her voice lowered. "Just be sure you are protected."

"Gerty!" Maeve gasped.

"I'm just saying. He's awfully good-looking, you know."

Maeve did know. Her cheeks burned. "That is not going to happen. If I thought it would, I'd be on the first plane home."

"Listen to me," Gerty ordered. "You've been in prison too long. If you get a chance to go crazy, well, by golly, you grab it. You deserve some joy, Maeve. If Chuck Lawrence can bring it to you, then he has my blessing."

"You've been reading too many romance novels, Gerty. Life doesn't work that way. I'm past all that." Voicing that sentiment as certainty, though, cast a further pall on the day.

"Well, you may be too old for romance, but I'm sure not," declared Gerty, who was only a few years older than Maeve.

"Oh, Gerty, I wish I had your spirit." Maeve's shoulders sagged.

"You got your own gumption, girl, whether you believe it or not. Do me one favor, all right?"

It wasn't often Gerty sounded so serious. "What?"

"Promise me first." When Maeve hesitated, she pushed. "Trust me, hon."

"All right." But Maeve felt certain she wouldn't like it.

"Go to Asheville. Forget Hilton, forget your kids—it's only four days. I'll call you if anyone needs you, but in the meantime, just relax. Let go. You're running on empty, Maeve. Refill the tank. Everything will still be here to deal with when you get back."

"That's what I'm afraid of. I can't afford to relax."

"You can't afford not to." Gerty went on without waiting for a response, "I'm calling your kids right now and telling them that you're taking a few days off."

"But what will they think if they find out I'm with Chuck?"

"They just might decide there's hope for you,

after all," Gerty said, chuckling. "At the very least, they'll have some reason to call each other and talk."

"Very funny." But Maeve knew Gerty was right. Her children didn't really need her, and it was past time for her to demonstrate that she would make it on her own. She exhaled. "All right, I'll go. But not for a fling, Gerty. I'm not the type."

"Well, maybe it's time you were."

"Does Chuck have you on his payroll?"

"He couldn't afford me. You have fun now, you hear?" There was a definite smile in her voice. "I want all the details when you get back."

"You wish." Maeve was smiling as she hung up the phone.

HE COULDN'T REMEMBER the last time he'd cared so much about a first impression. As they detoured off the main road approaching the hillside where his cabin stood, Chuck cast quick peeks at Maeve's face to see her reaction.

"Oh, I'd forgotten how much I love mountains." She'd rolled down the window and kept sticking her head out to sniff the air. "The scent of pines, the cool air. Why on earth do I live where it's hotter than Hades more than half the year?"

You can come here anytime, he wanted to say, but didn't dare. Instead, he murmured agreement as they rounded the last curve.

"Oh." She sat up straight, leaned forward. "Oh, that's…" Her eyes were wide. "Is this it?"

He nodded.

"Chuck, it's gorgeous." She placed her hands on the dash. "You said a cabin."

"It is." He rolled to a stop.

She was out of the car in a flash. "You're wrong. This…" She threw her arms wide and turned in a circle, her eyes taking in the clearing, the view from the side of the mountain. Then she smiled. "This is paradise."

"You haven't seen the inside yet."

"I don't need to. I think I'll just bring a blanket and sleep right here. Look at that." She nodded toward the valley that spilled out below them.

"Sunrise is really something," he agreed. "But the temperature drops a lot at night this time of year. You'll freeze that lovely fanny right off."

She tensed, and he reminded himself that this was a hands-off trip. If Maeve wanted to fool around, she would have to initiate it. "Come on." He held out a hand. "There's another deck that catches the sunset."

To his surprise, she accepted his grasp. "Shouldn't we get our bags and the groceries?"

"Later. It's cool enough that they'll be fine until you have the grand tour."

As they climbed the stairs to the first floor, he couldn't help a sense of pride as he saw the cabin through her eyes. He'd built this place after June died, needing to get out of Dallas and everything familiar for a while. He'd done much of the work himself, and the labor had been healing. Pounding nails and sweating were therapeutic. His sons and daughter had come to help him with various stages, and they sometimes used the place themselves. He liked the idea that maybe someday grandchildren would be visiting.

Maeve paced the large living room with its floor-to-ceiling windows overlooking the pasture below and the tree-covered slopes beyond. She trailed her fingers over the granite countertops in the spacious kitchen, and he felt the caress as if it were his own flesh.

She nodded in approval at the five bedrooms and three baths on the main floor, sparse as the decor might be. "You'd have done better with the interiors," he said before he thought.

She turned. "Your friend's taste is just fine. There's nothing wrong with simplicity."

He bit his tongue before he could reveal too much. "You're right. One more floor." He led her upstairs to his room, the one he'd never shared with a woman. Cecily was a city girl through and through, and there hadn't been anyone else he would have considered bringing here. He opened the door.

"It's huge." Her eyes widened. "I love these log walls. And this bed—wow!"

A massive four-poster, each post hewn from a separate tree felled when he'd cleared this spot, the bed faced an enormous picture window with the same stunning view as the living room, and a skylight lit the space from above. "The bath is through there," he indicated.

She hesitated. "I feel like a trespasser. This is obviously the owner's bedroom. I don't want to pry."

"He won't mind." Chuck led the way. There was nothing spartan about the bathroom with its steam shower standing beside an oversized clawfoot tub. Another skylight enhanced the golden glow of the walls.

Maeve pressed one hand to her throat. "If this was mine, I think I'd live here full-time. How can he stand to leave it?"

He used to get lonely here, Chuck thought. "He comes as often as he can." She filled up the empty spaces, just by being here. Chuck wasn't sure how to feel about that.

"Where's my room?" she asked.

"Take this one."

"Oh, no, I couldn't." But her eyes told a different story. "It would be invading his privacy. Disturbing his sanctuary."

She'd already done that. He hadn't found his equilibrium since the first day he'd visited the shelter.

"He'd want you to make yourself at home. It's his primary condition for letting us stay."

"Then you take this room."

Only if you're in it with me. He shook his head. "I already have dibs on the one with the king-size bed downstairs." The prime guest room, intended for couples. He'd outfitted the others to hold larger parties, including one with four sets of bunk beds. "Please, Maeve. Treat yourself."

She looked around her once more, greedily taking in the view. "All right. If you're sure."

"Absolutely." He took his first deep breath of the day. She was committed, at least for now. He had three more full days before they had to leave for Atlanta. He intended to make them count. "I'll go get the bags."

"Uh-uh," she said, skipping past him down the stairs. "Fifty-fifty, remember? Last one down's a—" He used his familiarity and his size to shoot past her, grabbing her around the waist as he leaped the last two steps "—rotten egg." He twirled her one time, reveling as she gripped his shoulders, giggling.

Then he set her down far sooner than he'd have liked. She remained where she was. He tightened his hands on her waist and bent to her, brushing her lips with his own when what he really wanted to do was scoop her up and head back to his bedroom. "Welcome, Maeve. I'm glad you've come." Then he carefully stepped back. "After you, partner."

She studied him thoughtfully, her eyes soft and confused as she turned away and preceded him down the last flight of stairs.

MAEVE AWOKE SLOWLY, trying to remember where she was. Golden beams overhead had her blinking. The bright blue sky of their arrival was a soft lavender now. She sat up quickly. How long had she slept?

She shoved herself to standing and had to grab the bedpost for support. She'd fallen asleep in her clothes and slept so deeply that her muscles still didn't want to move. She couldn't recall the last time she'd slept so well.

She made her way to the bathroom then decided to shower. She thought about just putting on her nightgown, but as she was pawing through her suitcase, she realized why the light was so different.

It was dawn, not twilight. Chuck had said these windows faced the sunrise.

She must have slept nearly twelve hours. She was mortified.

And yet, she felt the best she had in a very long time. Quickly she donned jeans and a sweater, wishing she'd brought thicker socks, as well. She returned to the bathroom and thanked her ancestors for the dark brows and eyelashes she'd been given. Deliberately, she left her other makeup where it was to test herself. She hadn't faced the world without makeup in forty years.

At the last second, she swiped on some lipstick, shaking her head at how difficult vanity was to elude completely.

She tiptoed down the stairs, not wanting to wake Chuck. He'd said there was no pressure on this trip, but surely he hadn't imagined his guest would not even make an appearance the first night.

When she reached the kitchen, she tried to recall where he'd said the coffee supplies were, then she spotted a note propped by the coffeemaker. *Just flip the switch. Everything's ready. Chuck*

He'd said he wasn't helpless in the kitchen. She

tried to imagine Hilton doing this, even *thinking* of it. As she waited for the coffee to perk, she peered in the refrigerator.

She was starving.

An apple would do the trick for now. She didn't want to make any unnecessary noise. She had no idea if Chuck was a late sleeper, but he deserved a vacation, too. When the coffee was finished, she poured a cup, then snagged a quilt off the sofa and made her way outside to the deck.

Sunrise. How she loved it. She made herself a nest in an Adirondack chair and settled in for the show. The air was chilly but sweet, crisp with the tang of pine. A squirrel ran across the ground where mist clung to the contours of the earth and hovered around the lower tree branches.

In the distance, the distinctive blue that gave these mountains their name undulated in wave after wave, from ashy blue to deepest charcoal.

Now if only Daniel Day-Lewis would charge through the woods bare-chested in front of her, the way he did in *The Last of the Mohicans*. Maeve snickered at herself.

A bird swooped by—oh, what was it? She hoped there was a field guide inside to help her identify it. She sipped her coffee, munched on her apple and fell head over heels in love with the morning.

CHUCK STOOD at the window and watched her, smiling at her delight. He wanted, more than he'd wanted anything in a long time, to join her.

But Maeve needed the peace as much as she'd needed the sleep.

So he forced himself to stay right where he was.

CHAPTER FOURTEEN

AN EARLY RISER, Chuck awoke on the second day with energy to burn. Maeve was still asleep—she'd done a lot of that yesterday. He didn't begrudge her; as the old saying went, you could have packed for a week in the bags beneath her eyes.

Not that he'd ever say so. He wasn't stupid. Besides, she wasn't one whit less attractive to him. Conversely, seeing her at ease, clad simply, with little makeup and her hair loose, he only wanted her more.

But he'd made a promise, one he didn't really regret, however eager he was for her to make the first move.

He fixed coffee and drank it, then slapped a piece of ham between two slices of bread, grabbed a bottle of water and went outside to chop wood. If he was lucky, he'd get blisters and *want* to keep his hands to himself.

Right.

He'd been hard at it for maybe an hour, plenty

long enough to work up a sweat and strip off his sweater, leaving only a plain white T-shirt beneath. His muscles were singing with the effort, and he was glad for every workout he'd forced himself to do on days when he'd rather have been doing anything else.

The back of his neck prickled with awareness. He swung the ax again to split one more log, then turned.

Maeve stood about ten feet away, two coffee mugs in her hands. "Would you rather have water?"

"No, thanks." He nodded at the bottle nearby, then crossed to her. "Did I wake you?" He took one mug as she shook her head. "Thanks." Black, just the way he liked it. "Lucky guess?" He gestured with the mug.

"I remember from the café…and from dinner at my place." Her violet eyes lifted to his.

"You look great. Rested."

She smoothed her hair then turned up one palm. "It's the real me, I'm afraid." She glanced around them. "Somehow, surrounded by such beauty, make-up and blow-dryers seem pointless."

"Beauty, indeed." But he wasn't looking at their surroundings, only at her. "Feel better?"

She smiled. "I do. I should apologize for sleeping so much."

"Please don't. It's why we're here."

We. Somehow the word sounded right.

She glanced up at him as if aware of the same idea. "Thank you for pushing me to make the trip."

Her cheeks reddened, and she looked away. "I sure haven't held up my end of our bargain."

"Want to make it up to me?" He cocked one eyebrow and grinned.

She delayed with a sip from her cup. "Do I dare ask how?" Her lips curved.

"Oh, sweetheart, you don't want to open that door."

But she surprised him. "Maybe..." she began, then halted. "Never mind."

"Uh-uh." He bent to her. "Finish your sentence."

"I don't think so." She put some distance between them. "I'm going to make you a lumberjack breakfast."

"Coward." He said it with a smile, though.

"Maybe." But her eyes were sparkling. "I'll call you when it's ready, unless you come in sooner."

He'd like to, he'd really like to.

But he'd better burn off some more energy, instead.

SHE'D MADE HIM a breakfast that some called a widow-maker, all the bad stuff in one meal— sausage, biscuits slathered with butter, eggs...the works. A steady diet of such food wouldn't be good, but Chuck was obviously fit—very fit, as his sweaty T-shirt attested—and he'd wolfed it down.

She would be thinking about how he looked in that T-shirt and worn jeans hugging his long legs and very fine behind for a very long time.

Though she'd cooked, she'd insisted that she still

owed on her fifty percent, so she'd meant to clean up the kitchen alone.

But he'd lingered for another cup of coffee and somehow sneakily done quite a bit of that cleaning.

Then he'd lured her outside for a walk in the woods. Fully awake for the first time since they'd arrived, she was alive to every second, the magic of the place seeping into her pores. Bars of sunlight drifted through the trees, dusting the tops of the underbrush. The fall colors were a glorious tapestry of gold and yellow and bronze. A notion struck her, and she began picking up the best specimens of leaves.

"What are you doing?"

"I want to make a gift for the owner, a thank-you. It won't be nearly enough, but the person who could build this amazing place might appreciate what I have in mind."

An odd look crossed his face.

"What? You think I'm wrong?"

He shook his head. "No. Knowing your creativity, I bet the owner will treasure it."

His tone was husky, and a little shiver ran through her. "I hope so," was all she could manage. "I don't know what to do for you, though, to thank you." She caught a glimpse of his mock-leer and laughed. "Besides that, I mean."

He slapped a hand over his heart. "You're killing me, Maeve."

She sobered. "I'm sorry."

He snagged her hand and brought it to his lips. "Don't be. I can take it."

His warm breath over her palm, softly blown through her fingers, made her shiver again. His gaze went to her lips.

He was such a good man.

He would be an amazing lover, too, she was sure of it. Not that she had any experience other than with Hilton.

But wasn't lovemaking about consideration as much as heat? About kindness? Attentiveness?

Chuck generated heat, in spades, but more than that, he'd been so caring of her. She still had no idea why her, really.

You deserve some joy, Maeve, Gerty had said. *If Chuck Lawrence can bring it to you, then he has my blessing.*

He could. She knew he could. And she was more than a little tempted to let him.

"Chuck," she began, then bit her lip. Was she really ready for such a big step?

"Yes?" His gray eyes locked on hers.

You've been in prison too long. If you get a chance to go crazy, well, by golly, you grab it.

"Kiss me," she blurted.

He blinked. "What did you say?"

"You heard me."

His brows snapped together. "Why?"

"What do you care?"

"I'm not sure you're ready," he said carefully.

Maeve stared at him. "Excuse me, but haven't we been dancing around this for weeks now? Or were you only teasing me?"

His gaze went hot. He took one step forward but didn't touch her.

If she had to wait any longer, she'd scream. Or run.

By golly, you grab it. Surprising herself, Maeve closed the gap. Kissed *him,* instead.

Chuck hesitated for a fraction…

Then hauled her into his arms and laid a kiss on her that had her toes curling. Leaves fluttered from her fingers, then she wrapped her arms around his neck…

And returned the favor.

Maeve swirled her tongue over his lips, and he groaned.

"Don't tempt me, sugar."

Her hands slid into his hair. She opened her mouth to his.

Moaned. Wriggled against him.

"Our first time won't be on a forest floor," he muttered as his hands wandered.

She pressed closer. Let her own hands roam over that wonderful, muscular body.

"That's it. I'm only giving you an hour to stop. If you refuse, the consequences could be serious." Chuck grinned, but his face was strained. "I knew you'd be like this," he murmured. "You give a first impression of being prim, when in reality you could drive a man mad." He nuzzled behind her ear and had her purring.

"Gerty told me I should go crazy," she said breathlessly as his mouth traveled down her throat.

"I knew I loved that woman."

All at once, he swung Maeve up into his arms and strode toward the house.

She gasped, then clung. Stroked his chest. Kissed his neck, nibbled his ear.

"Behave yourself," he ordered. Then his eyebrows waggled. "On second thought, don't."

Maeve shivered.

AFTERNOON GAVE WAY TO NIGHT, and Maeve experienced for the first time in her life what lovemaking could be when pleasure was not bartered, when power was shared…when tenderness was the currency.

In those hours, she forgot that her body was aging, that her problems were many, that her resources were few. Chuck was a man accustomed to command, a man who wielded power every day. He could have controlled this experience, as well, but he gave her a gift that was priceless. Depths of pleasure she'd never imagined.

Maeve had borne four children, but though she loved them with everything in her, they did not originate from joy and certainly not from playfulness. Hilton was building an empire, and he needed heirs. Their births and lives had revolved around his ambitions.

But Chuck Lawrence was secure in who he was, a man who understood his place in the world and liked it just fine. He was strong enough to let go.

The night was a revelation in so many ways she'd lost count.

AS MORNING CREPT into the master bedroom, she tried to lie still, but the body stretched out beside her was far too fascinating. Memories of all they'd done together in the darkness swirled around her like genies whispering promises of untold riches. Sublime pleasures.

If she stayed here, she'd start touching him, and Chuck had had very little sleep. The same applied to her, too, but at the moment her skin was practically bursting from the energy trapped inside. As an act of mercy, she left him slumbering.

Downstairs, she wandered, planning in her head what she'd make him for breakfast, how they would spend their last full day together.

She frowned. The last day. Barely more than twenty-four hours left before she had to return to the real world, to her real life. This lovely respite would be over.

She would miss him so much. Her heart turned over at the thought of saying goodbye. Yes, they lived in the same town, but there were her children to consider, and his reputation. Hers, too, or whatever she could salvage of it.

And the financial problems, so many of which she must handle on her own.

He would help you.

She shoved away the treacherous temptation. He would, she was certain. For a moment, a very long moment, she let herself imagine what a relief it would be. He was so competent, so powerful. He could fix it, all of it, she was certain.

And she would absolutely love to see him do it.

Love. The word galvanized her, the power of it, the lure. She had a bone-deep yearning for it.

With a man such as Chuck.

Because, she realized, she could so easily love him back.

But what did she really know about true affection between a man and a woman? Her parents' marriage was based on ambition and status, and however much she had tried to avoid it, her own had wound up replicating exactly what she had most dreaded. Now she was reaping the harvest.

Fear was the wrong motive for anything—a life, a relationship. She could not allow herself to make another mistake.

What, after all, did she really know about Chuck? What, for that matter, did she know about herself?

And how on earth would she ever learn to stand on her own if she took the easy way out now?

She needed to write all of this down, fix it in black and white, like New Year's resolutions—only these revelations she had to keep, had to commit her mistakes to memory so she would never, ever forget them. Never backslide.

She opened drawers until she found one with odd bits of paper and rubber bands and broken pencils, searching for one clean sheet, one sharp point. As she rifled through the contents, one sheet with writing on it fell out, and she bent to retrieve it.

It was an invoice from Appalachian Butane. And it was billed to Charles Lawrence, owner. She frowned.

When the truth hit her, she gasped. Her chest tightened with breath she couldn't catch.

It belongs to someone I know, he'd said. *Nothing fancy.*

But this place was *his.* He'd lied to her. *Lied*—just as Hilton had done for years.

Also like Hilton, he'd decided what was right for her. Just as he had with Howard Sampson. Obviously he hadn't trusted her to come if she'd known that this place was his. That he was extending another act of charity.

Anger simmered, but beneath it was heartache, raw and bleeding. He didn't trust her. Didn't actually believe she could find her way out of any of this. If he did, he wouldn't keep propping her up.

She fought the urge to sink to the floor, to curl up in defeat. That was her way, had been her way for a long time.

Too long. Maeve hoarded her anger, tended it as one nurtured the first spark springing up in tinder, urging it to catch the kindling and burst into full flame. She hunched over, staring sightlessly as she prayed for her fury to scorch away all the longing, the foolish weakness that had led her to fall into bed with this man, to wish for him to take all her cares away.

She forced herself to think, and she outlined the steps in her head. She had to leave—now. Maybe one day she would be able to resist his charm, but her record was dismal thus far. Her only hope was to get away and clear her head of dreams and fantasies about love and tomorrows. Her real tomorrows would require all the logic and focus and strength she'd ever had, and more.

She eyed the car keys where he'd tossed them on the table beside the door. She didn't dare go pack— he was in her room.

His room, she realized, choking back tears. His bed, all along. His place, so breathtakingly beautiful. She allowed herself a moment to mourn all that had been lost here.

Then she ruthlessly switched her attention to what she had gained from this experience, a clear-eyed recognition that there was no one she could depend on really, except herself.

She blessed the fact that she'd left her purse downstairs. She would be cold without a jacket, but she would warm up in the car. She would find her way back to the last little town they'd passed on the way, and she would leave his vehicle there. Make arrangements for it to be returned.

She desperately wanted to go home, but her sons were expecting her in Atlanta, and Atlanta was closer, anyway. She would call Gerty and get her to send some clothes—and somehow she would make sure her children never knew how foolish their mother had been.

First things first, though. She left the butane bill on the counter and scribbled Chuck a fast note on a scrap of paper she found.

She didn't look around as she left. She couldn't bear any reminders of what she'd thought she'd found…what, instead, she had lost.

THE SOUND of an engine starting woke Chuck. He stirred and rolled over, already reaching for Maeve with a slow smile on his face.

Her side of the bed was empty. The sheets, cold. He sat up, raked fingers through his hair. "Maeve?"

No response.

Then he heard a vehicle driving off. He frowned and rose. Yanked on his jeans and grabbed a shirt, heading down the stairs barefoot.

Halfway down, he peered out the window over the door.

His SUV was gone from its parking spot. "Maeve?" he called, though already he could feel the dull thud of his heartbeat speeding up. She didn't know her way around these mountains. What could she have needed that couldn't wait?

He glanced around quickly. Spotted the paper on the counter.

Hesitated, as a bad feeling grew.

He grabbed the note. Saw first what was beneath it, the bill from the butane company. With his name on it.

He held the note up in the pale dawn light.

Please don't call or try to see me. Last night was a mistake.

I'll get your car back to you soon.

Maeve Branch

She'd signed her last name, as if they were only polite strangers. As if she wasn't already lodged in his heart. It was a slap in the face.

He'd known she might be upset that this place belonged to him, but after she fell in love with it, he'd thought she'd be happy to know she was welcome here anytime. He'd intended to tell her. The time just hadn't been right.

Please don't call or try to see me.

The *please* didn't mute the blow she'd delivered, the clear message that they were through when they'd barely begun.

He was not a man accustomed to taking orders. Hadn't he given her all kinds of room? Hadn't he catered to her concerns, soothed her fears? Granted her far more leeway than he ever did anyone in business? And how had she rewarded him?

She'd hurt him, damn it. He rubbed the heel of one hand against his chest. He'd been careful, ever since June's death, never to make himself vulnerable to anyone but his children. Then he'd stumbled across this complicated woman who'd done nothing but wreak havoc in the life he'd had solidly under control. Maeve was nothing but a mass of insecurities and a whole lot of trouble, yet somehow he'd gotten swept away. Opened himself to her as he'd never imagined he could, and what did she do but slip a knife right between his ribs.

Yet even as he seethed, he couldn't help worrying. Where was she going? Did she have any money? Why hadn't she taken her clothes?

He grabbed his PDA phone and scrolled to the number for the onboard guidance system of his car. He could have the vehicle tracked and get someone to make sure she was safe. Arrange for a ride for her, a flight to Atlanta—

I don't want charity.

I'm not helpless.

I need to be alone.

He stopped what he was doing, let the hand with the phone fall to his side.

Maybe she was right. Perhaps they needed some distance. However much it went against the grain to abandon her, maybe, just maybe, she was correct about that.

Last night was a mistake.

About that, however, they would never agree.

He lifted his phone again and called his pilot. Rubbed his breastbone some more as he waited to make arrangements to return to Dallas, to his real life, the one she'd interrupted.

A life that had been full until the day their paths had crossed at the shelter.

A life that now seemed as gray as the clouds moving in overhead.

CHAPTER FIFTEEN

"GREAT JOB, WILL!" shouted his crew chief, Seth
Gallant, over the radio. He turned to Maeve, seated
beside him in the pit box in honor of her upcoming
birthday. "I love that boy," Seth said. "Did you see
that side draft? Slicker than a whistle! If we'd had
another couple of laps, I think he could have won."

Maeve was grinning ear to ear. Will had come
in second, while Bart had been fifth. Rafael
O'Bryan had won for the second week in a row and
was on top in points, but when Maeve studied the
points standings, Will had moved up to seventh,
and Bart hadn't lost a spot. He was still sixth. Kent
Grosso was second, followed by his father, Dean,
in third, Justin Murphy in fourth and Hart
Hampton in fifth.

Just then, she saw the familiar gold-and-black
paint scheme of Will's No. 467 Ford roll down pit
road, where reporters were waiting to catch him. She
rose and removed her headphones while searching
for Bart's red-and-orange No. 475 car. "Thank you,
Seth. This was a treat."

"Anytime, Mrs. Branch. And happy birthday. What does this make? Thirty-six?"

She smiled past the ache in her heart. "Since Will is thirty, that might raise some eyebrows, but thanks for the compliment. You go on now. I know you all want to get on the plane."

He hesitated. "You're not going with us?"

She shook her head, relieved to be flying commercial this time. She wanted desperately to be alone. The charade she'd been conducting the whole time she'd been at Atlanta, smiling and convincing everyone she was just dandy, was taking its toll. "I'll catch him before he boards, though, but I need to see Bart first."

"I'll tell Will. He understands the system. Got to console the loser first."

She shook her finger at him. "A top-five finish isn't a loser."

"To Bart it will be, since Will got second. Thanks for being his good-luck charm. That Candy…" Seth shook his head over Will's current girlfriend, who'd decided to jet off to the Bahamas on short notice.

Maeve nodded. "I hear you." She wasn't too fond of the girl herself, but Candy hadn't lasted. None of them ever did. The girl who landed a Branch twin had her work cut out for her. Before Hilton's betrayal, they'd simply been high-spirited bachelors, but their father's desertion and their sister's once-troubled marriage had turned them into cynics about love and marriage.

She squeezed her eyes shut. After the disastrous trip to Asheville, she couldn't really blame them. How could her sons recognize true love when their mother was such a bad example?

Just then, she spotted Bart's car pulling in and shook off her grim thoughts. Her boys had done well today, and neither was mathematically out of the Chase.

Time to paste on one more convincing smile and go be a mother. It was the only part of being a woman she was any good at.

Thank heaven next week's race was at Texas.

She couldn't wait to get home.

CHUCK HIT THE OFF BUTTON on his plasma TV. For some masochistic reason, he hadn't been able to ignore the race, even though he was back home and football was on at the same time.

He'd gotten a shutter-quick glimpse of Maeve in Will's pit box when the TV announcers were interviewing Will's crew chief during a caution. He'd swung between wanting to freeze the frame to see how she was doing and getting angry all over again.

He just wasn't sure if he was more furious with her or with himself. For not telling her who owned the cabin, for getting involved too fast with a woman who was anything but ready, for still wishing he could find a way to fix everything in her life.

He tossed the remote onto the table and rose. He wasn't accustomed to being so restless. He hadn't slept well since he'd returned. He wondered if Maeve had.

It didn't matter. Whatever seedling had been un-curling and pushing through the soil had shriveled in the glare of all her problems and his…okay, his deceit.

Hell. It hadn't seemed that important that she know the cabin was his. Her need to know had been outweighed by his determination that she should find peace, even for a few days.

He picked up a stack of unanswered correspon-dence and rifled through it for a distraction. When he got to an invitation printed on a card, his fingers stilled.

It was to the annual charity auction for the animal shelter. Maeve had told him she meant to force herself to attend it as yet another step back into life. They'd mentioned going to it together, but had never made firm plans. It was in two days, on Tuesday night.

What if…

Please don't call or try to see me.

How could he leave her to do this alone? Would she tackle it by herself?

She was still in Atlanta.

But Gerty was not.

He picked up the phone and started dialing.

TUESDAY EVENING Maeve held the phone to her ear while she glanced at the clock. "Mom," Penny said. "Did you hear me?"

"I did, and I'm so happy for you and Craig. Very soon you'll be parents."

"If the birth mother doesn't change her mind. It's all I can think about."

"Has she said something?"

"No, it's just that—" Penny's voice broke "—after all we've been through and how I never believed I'd get to be a mother...we're so close, and every day I get more frightened that we'll be denied."

"I can certainly understand your worry, sweetheart, but worrying accomplishes nothing. It only keeps you from enjoying this special time, the anticipation."

"I know you're right." Penny exhaled as if laying down a burden. "I have so much to be thankful for, with Craig back in my life. I love him so much, and sometimes it just seems like there should be a price for being this happy."

"If that's so—and I don't really believe it—then haven't you and Craig paid plenty up front? You nearly lost each other. It was a terrible time for you both."

"It was." Maeve heard the tears in her daughter's voice.

"Mom, I could still change clothes and come get you, if you're determined to attend the auction. Craig and I both would be happy to escort you."

Maeve smiled. "As would your brothers—even Sawyer offered to fly in. Halfway across the country, can you imagine?"

"We love you. We'd do anything to help."

Maeve's eyes misted. "I know you would, honey, but I have to do this myself." However terrified she was. "Now if you want to conjure up the perfect outfit, I won't quibble."

"I thought you were wearing that lavender Carolina Herrera that's always looked so great on you."

Maeve stared into the mirror at the very dress they were discussing. "Nothing looks great on me anymore." Then she bit her lip. Discussing her insecurities would accomplish nothing. "Oh, don't listen to me. I'm just nervous. I'll be fine." Her stomach was a tangle of epic proportions. She hadn't been able to eat since breakfast.

"You will be, you know. You're stronger than you give yourself credit for, Mom. You're my inspiration."

"Me?" Maeve blinked. "I've been a doormat most of my life."

"You have not. Oh, I don't say that Daddy didn't strut around like he ruled the roost, but who kept our lives going while he was preening? Who devoted herself to her children and made each of us feel like we could accomplish anything we wanted? Mom, you couldn't be more wrong. You might have let him have sway on financial matters, but at home it was you who provided the safe place where we all knew we could come when the world got too scary."

Maeve couldn't speak for a minute around the

lump in her throat. "Oh, sweetheart…" She sniffed and reached for a tissue. "Now you're going to cause me to ruin my makeup." She dabbed carefully at her eyes. "Thank you for that. I—I don't know what to say." But then she did. "I've made a lot of mistakes in my life, but I promise you this—I'm done hiding and letting others take over." She took a deep breath. "So I'm going there tonight in my lavender dress, and whether or not I look dressed to kill, I'm going to be a killer in my heart. I'll swat away all those pitying glances, and I'll hold my head high." She paused. "I'm going to remember my gorgeous daughter who wanted to throw up before every runway show and how she always made it look easy when she stepped from behind the curtain."

"Never let them see you sweat, that's what you taught us, Mom."

"I used to be good at projecting an image," Maeve said. "Guess it's time I sharpened my skills."

"You'll knock them dead, I'm absolutely positive."

Maeve straightened as she glanced in the mirror. Icy, Chuck had called her. That was what he'd thought.

Oh, dear God, if he was there tonight—

No. Forget him. And *icy* is good.

"Butter won't melt in my mouth," Maeve told her daughter, even as her fingers twisted in her skirt.

"Go get 'em, tiger," Penny said. "And never forget how much we love you."

"I won't," Maeve whispered, and finished saying goodbye.

Then she grabbed her purse and marched down the stairs like a prisoner facing execution.

"SO WHAT WILL YOU be bidding on this evening?" Cecily asked Chuck.

He glanced down at his uncomplicated companion. Being with Cecily was so…easy. She had her own money and treasured her independence. She was bright and interesting and beautiful, to boot.

She just wasn't Maeve. He stirred himself to answer. "See anything you'd like?"

"A smile on your face would be nice." Her gaze ranged over him. "What's troubling you, Chuck?"

"Nothing." He glanced away, then froze.

Maeve stood in the doorway of the ballroom. She had her ice-queen face on, but he wondered if anyone else saw the fear in her frame. As he watched, she drew herself up into full composure, but he knew what had to be going on inside her.

He took an involuntary step forward, then stopped as Bart and Will crossed to greet her.

Good for you, Gerty, asking the twins to come to Dallas early. Okay, Maeve would be furious if she knew the part he'd played—but she wouldn't. Gerty had promised. If Maeve wouldn't let him protect her, he couldn't simply stand aside, so he'd enlisted Gerty to make sure Maeve wasn't alone.

The smile that lit up her face told her he'd been

right to meddle. She'd proved her point by coming here alone, but now her sons flanked her, tall and handsome and strong. Maeve circled the room between them, every inch the queen as she graciously greeted the members of her social set with nary a quiver to betray her.

Good for you, sweetheart. Good for you.

Then the crowd parted, and one of the twins— he thought it was Bart—spotted him and began to bring her over. "Hey, Chuck." Bart extended a hand, smiling...

Until he spotted Cecily holding on to Chuck's arm.

Just about then, Maeve noticed them, too. Introductions were performed, but he was barely aware of a single word he uttered. Instead, he tried to hold her gaze, to communicate words he couldn't say in public. Words like *I'm sorry* and *Are you okay?* and *I'm proud of you.*

Along with *I love you.* And *please let me explain.*

But her eyes had already shifted to Cecily, and she froze.

The twins kept looking from their mother to him, to Cecily and back, and the moment was awkward as hell. How did he explain, especially in the middle of this crowd? Particularly when he would do anything to avoid causing Maeve more pain.

So he seized on the race. "Great race, guys, both of you. You're still in the hunt."

But the atmosphere had cooled drastically in seconds.

Will's expression was stormy. Bart's was more composed and Chuck could see how aware Maeve's son was of the need to avoid further upset. Her knuckles were white where she gripped Will's arm.

So Bart took over smoothly, thanking him, telling Cecily it was nice to meet her and getting Maeve away as soon as he could.

While Will glared at him over Maeve's head.

It took everything Chuck had not to storm over, yank her from her sons' grip and spirit her away somewhere that they could be alone and she couldn't run from him again. Where he could explain, and she would listen and understand. Where they could turn back the clock to the most incredible night of his life.

Jaw clenching, he tore his gaze away before he could act.

"Want to talk about what just happened?" Cecily asked.

He looked at her, but all he could see was Maeve's devastation. "No." He forced himself to relax. "I'm sorry." He had to get away, clear his head. "Want more champagne?"

Her eyes were sympathetic. "Sure."

"Be right back." Simmering with pent-up rage, Chuck cut through the crowd.

WELL, HE HADN'T waited long, had he? Maeve made her way to the ladies' room, having excused herself from her sons to regain her composure.

It didn't matter. Nothing mattered except getting

through this night. She began to calculate exactly how quickly she could leave—

She nearly stumbled over a woman in her path. "Pardon me," she said perfunctorily and began to skirt around.

The woman shifted so she was right in front of Maeve. "Well, well, well. The little mouse finally comes out of hiding."

Maeve's head jerked up, and she stared straight into the eyes of Alyssa Ritchie, Hilton's mistress. The junior architect of her agony, the author of the tell-all book that claimed Maeve was only half a woman, unable to satisfy her man.

Everyone around them froze. Maeve could almost hear the collective intake of breath.

Maeve's first inclination was to run, but she surprised herself with a surge of pure rage. It was all she could do not to slap the woman's botoxed face. She was rocked by the urge to claw, to shriek, to yank that bottle-blond hair out by the roots.

And she could tell that Alyssa knew it, too. The only difference was that Alyssa would welcome a catfight. A messy confrontation would only sell more books.

Never let them see you sweat.

While everyone around her waited for Maeve to cower or to fight or maybe even—joy of joys—weep, Maeve found within herself the astonishing ability to do something utterly unexpected, even to herself.

She smiled. Simply smiled, her expression dripping with pity much like that which had come her way so often recently, though doing so required everything she had. Then with all the dignity she could summon, she held her head high and moved on, speaking, instead, to the first person she recognized, as if Alyssa Ritchie were less than a speck of dirt on her shoe and not worth a single word.

WHAT A WOMAN.

Chuck had heard the hush fall over the room and turned just in time to see Alyssa Ritchie plant herself in Maeve's path, her expression that of a cat with a particularly tasty morsel in her grasp. He looked for Will or Bart, but they, too, were far away from the scene. He tried to shove his way toward her, but the crowd would not part. He could only stand and watch and be grateful for the height that gave him a clear view.

There couldn't be many in the room who hadn't heard Alyssa's challenge. She'd told him she had no real friends in their social circles, but he hadn't really believed it.

He did now. Everyone appeared to have bought into the image he'd once mistaken for the truth of who Maeve Branch was and be greedily awaiting her downfall.

He redoubled his efforts and managed to edge his way a few feet closer, but he couldn't get to her in time. He tried to catch her eye, but she had that mask solidly planted over her features. So when she put

Alyssa in her place so deftly, with a demonstration of grace and composure the highest-ranking diplomat would envy, all he could do was smile and mentally tip his hat.

I was right, Maeve. You're stronger than you know.

He was so proud of her in that moment that he could no longer acquiesce to the plea in the note she'd left. He had to reach her, to tell her. To be with her so she would know she wasn't alone.

He took a step forward, only to find his path blocked. He glanced down to excuse himself…and looked straight into the eyes of the very woman Maeve had just scorned. "Excuse me, Alyssa," he said, and tried to go around her.

"How are you, Chuck?" Alyssa's eyes were bright with fury, but that didn't deter her from the sex-kitten purr that was her trademark. She laid her hand on his arm and tilted her head, perusing him from beneath unnaturally thick eyelashes in her coquette's practiced move.

"I'm fine. If you'll excuse me—" He took a step away, but she held on.

"I see you're here with Cecily," she continued, her jaw clenched. "But I do believe I've heard rumors about you and the Virgin Queen having dinner at La Mireille. Surely you can do better." She spread her fingers over his chest.

He clamped his hand over her wrist. "Leave Maeve alone, Alyssa."

"My, my." Her eyes widened. "A knight to the rescue, is it?" She shook her head. "Didn't you read my book, darling? She can't keep a man happy in bed."

You couldn't be more wrong, he thought. He stepped away and caught motion in the corner of his eye.

Maeve stood in the doorway, looking straight at him, her expression stricken.

Then she turned away.

No! He wrested himself from Alyssa's grasp and plunged into the crowd after Maeve.

Before he could, Bart planted himself squarely in Chuck's way. Over Bart's shoulder, Chuck saw Will escort Maeve outside.

"What's going on, Lawrence?" Bart demanded. "What are you doing with that tramp? Why are you hurting my mother?"

Chuck could see ears perking up nearby. "Let's go outside. I need to talk to Maeve." He tried to go around the younger man, but Bart wasn't budging.

"No. You explain yourself. Hasn't she been through enough?"

"I'm not her problem," Chuck insisted. "And we can't discuss this here." He jerked his head to indicate the interested stares. "Anyway, she's the one I need to be talking to."

"Not until we talk first," Bart insisted. "But you're right. Not here. And not tonight. Will and I need to get her home."

"I'll follow you."

"No," Bart said. He thought for a second. "Come to the track tomorrow. I'm doing a charity ride-along, but I'll be done by noon. Meet me in the garage area. You won't need a pass until Thursday."

Everything in Chuck strained to fight Maeve's son on this. He and she needed to clear the air. He didn't like one bit having to wait.

But Bart was not a child, and he was clearly determined. Alienating Maeve's children was no way to win her heart.

"All right," he said reluctantly. "But then I'm going to see Maeve, and there's not a damn thing you can do to stop me."

"Don't bet on it." The younger man's expression was grim, and Chuck reminded himself that Bart wasn't easily frightened, given what he did for a living.

"You don't understand what's going on between us," Chuck said.

"No," Bart responded, a muscle in his jaw jumping. "But you can be damn sure I will tomorrow." He wheeled and left the room.

Chuck took a second to calm himself. Cecily approached. "Apparently I missed the show." Her smile vanished as Chuck turned to her. "Talk to me, Chuck. What's going on?"

He could only shake his head. "It's complicated."

She touched his forearm. "Not from where I stand." Her gaze was fond. "You don't have to talk if you don't want to—what's happening is pretty clear. You're in love with her. I'm happy for you."

"I wish *I* could be. She told me to get lost."

"Oh, my. But you know she doesn't mean it, don't you?"

"I hurt her, Cecily. All I wanted to do was help her."

She patted his arm. "The course of true love seldom runs smooth."

"Don't sound so cheerful. I don't know how to fix it."

Cecily nodded. "Men forever want to fix things. It's not always possible. She's had a lot thrown at her, Chuck. Remember that patience you assured me you had plenty of?"

"Don't remind me," he grumbled.

Cecily glanced around them. "I believe I'm bored with this gathering. How about you? I think I'll make an early night of it."

He smiled at her fondly. "You're a good person, you know that? I can stick it out until the auction."

Her smile was equally fond. "No, I don't really think you can. Take me home, so you can go brood." They turned to go, but she halted. "I do wish you well, Chuck." She stood on tiptoe and kissed his cheek. "She'll be worth it in the end."

"Yeah," he said, and escorted her out the door.

MAEVE THOUGHT she would never get the boys to let her go to bed. Normally she was thrilled to have any of her children back home again, but tonight she desperately wanted to be alone. Convincing them that she was all right, preventing their simmering anger from exploding and impelling them to do something foolish required everything she had.

They were prepared to storm over to Chuck's with their fists, and they also badly wanted to make Alyssa pay somehow for the spectacle she'd incited. Even the hazard of jeopardizing their position in the Chase for the NASCAR Sprint Cup wasn't enough to dissuade them.

Finally she'd resorted to pleading for herself, something she loathed doing. Only the prospect of making her life more miserable stopped them. They weren't happy about leaving either Chuck or Alyssa alone, but she'd wrested a promise from them to at least not leave the house tonight.

So at last she was alone in her room, exhausted, but far too overwrought to sleep.

A hundred images of the night assaulted her, but surprisingly, the confrontation with Alyssa was not the most disturbing. Though Maeve had been shaking inside like a bowl of half-set gelatin, she was proud of how she'd handled the woman. You didn't win by climbing into the mud with someone like that. Alyssa was shaken by Maeve's refusal to give her credence, and the knowledge bought back a tiny fragment of Maeve's badly damaged self-esteem.

No, it was Chuck who starred in her misery, above the crowd of extras in tonight's horror film. She'd learned long ago to close herself off from others in those sorts of social situations. It was how a shy girl had survived life in a prominent family and, later, endured her husband's demands and pretensions.

But she had no armor for Chuck. Seeing him smiling and happy with Cecily Dunstan had been bad enough. He sure hadn't mourned long over losing her, had he?

Even Cecily and how obviously he enjoyed her company was nothing, though, compared to seeing that witch Alyssa's hand on his chest, regardless that logic told her Alyssa was only striking back. She didn't want that woman's hands on her man, the muscled body that had held Maeve so tenderly, made love so sweetly.

At last, her control broke. One sob erupted, then another. Soon, Maeve was curled up on her bed, weeping into her pillow. Crying her heart out over what had been building between them, and what had been lost with the discovery that he'd lied to her.

Illusions. Would she never stop building castles of sand? She hurt so badly…would it never stop? Would she never reach the end of this darkness Hilton's actions had cast her into?

Hilton's an asshole, she could hear Chuck saying, and at the memory, the unthinkable happened.

She stopped crying. However badly things had ended between her and Chuck, she had learned from him, too. That was the trick, wasn't it, to learn from every experience?

You are anything but stupid, Maeve. Blind, maybe, perhaps even willfully so, but you can change that if you're willing to work at it.

She sat up in the bed. She had been blind and foolish, but she'd done something good tonight. Taken an important step in facing down Alyssa.

So what was the next step?

Hilton's an asshole. Maeve smiled and repeated it out loud.

Then she knew her next move. She'd dealt with Hilton's mistress, but she'd dodged Hilton himself. It was time to lay things to rest between them. She wasn't sure what she wanted exactly—an apology from Hilton or the opportunity to show him she would survive despite him? She really didn't know, and the uncontested divorce meant she never had to see him again—but she realized she needed to put a period on their life together. Avoiding him would never do that.

Maeve rose and looked back at where she'd lain in a puddle of misery on a bed that was not her own, a bed she'd retreated to because she couldn't face the room she'd shared with Hilton.

She'd dodged too many challenges in the past several months, but the few she'd faced made her feel a stirring of pride, and that was food to a starving soul.

It wouldn't be easy, and she didn't kid herself that she wasn't scared half to death at the prospect of seeing Hilton again.

It was another step in a journey the end of which she couldn't see yet. Might not see for a very long time.

She would take a leap of faith and try once more to move ahead.

CHAPTER SIXTEEN

CHUCK USED the half-hour drive to the race track to get his day in order. He'd been giving his business short shrift ever since Maeve appeared on his radar and consumed too much of his attention. He'd assembled a very competent staff, but there had to be a captain at the helm of any ship. This captain couldn't afford much more shore leave.

But Maeve was important. Too important, perhaps, for his own peace of mind. And now he had to play territorial games with her sons.

Not that he blamed them. In their shoes, he'd be all over anyone who'd hurt her. And they were not boys but men.

He wheeled up to the security gate and marveled at how enormous this facility was, set out in the countryside nearer Fort Worth than Dallas. He'd heard somewhere that the speedway was huge, even by Texas standards.

The grounds were already full of campers and tents. Race fans didn't just show up on the day of the event—a NASCAR weekend was really a week-long party for the faithful, who arrived long before the NASCAR Craftsman Truck Series or the NASCAR Nationwide Series races began. Today was Wednesday, the day before the haulers arrived, yet there were already booths set up, flags flying from antennae, barbecue grills smoking. The honorees of the party hadn't yet arrived, but their guests were warming things up.

As Chuck waited for the guard to confirm that he was indeed an invited visitor to the Branch brothers, he found himself smiling at the sea of campers whose numbers would swell dramatically in the next two days.

He was hooked on NASCAR, he might as well admit it. There was something about NASCAR that got into your blood. He refused to believe that he would not find a way to resolve things with Maeve, but regardless, this sport had snared him. If he couldn't win Maeve's love, he might not want to be at a track again because of the memories of her, but he'd have to know how her sons' careers proceeded, would want to watch on TV, at least.

That realization made him more patient with the confrontation to come. He was every bit as proud of Maeve's sons for sticking up for her as he was aggravated by the obstacle they presented.

So when he wheeled into the assigned parking spot and saw Will stalking toward him, still obviously furious, Chuck tamped down his own territorial urges and emerged from his SUV with his hand outstretched. "How are you, Will?"

Will ignored the handshake. Jerked his head toward pit road. "Bart's finishing his last ride."

Chuck dug deep for that elusive patience and simply responded, "Fine." They walked in silence through the garage area, so quiet and empty in contrast to how it would look when tomorrow arrived.

Bart rolled into a pit stall, and his last ride hopped out, a teenager who was a little pale but also bursting with excitement. Bart visited with him a little longer, paused for the boy's dad to take pictures of the two of them together, then at last excused himself and walked over, helmet in hand, hair plastered to his head with sweat. "Lawrence," he acknowledged.

"Bart." Chuck nodded.

"I thought we'd take a ride." His eyebrows rose. "If you're game."

Ah. So that was how it would be. *We'll put the old guy in his place by scaring the living daylights out of him.* Chuck saw the brothers exchange a smirk, expecting him to demur.

"Great. Where's my helmet?" What they didn't credit was that Chuck had a healthy appetite for adrenaline rushes himself—and he hadn't always been an old guy. A roughneck's life wasn't sunshine and roses, and when you were out on a rig in the middle of the ocean during a hurricane, you couldn't afford to get rattled. When he'd started making money, he'd done the usual guy things, at least until he had children and June had begged him to slow down on the skydiving and BASE jumping, the rock climbing and scuba diving.

"You'll need a uniform," Will said. "Good thing we're both tall. Most drivers' gear wouldn't fit you. I've got one of mine in the motor home."

Other drivers' motor homes wouldn't arrive until later, but because Will and Bart were doing a special charity function before NASCAR's tenancy began, they'd had theirs show up early. Chuck followed Will and cataloged for the first time the similarities in their frames. Hilton hadn't been that tall, and Maeve sure wasn't. Somewhere, however, height had been passed down to them, since both were, as Will had noted, much taller than the normal driver, who was more likely to be five-foot-eight than their six-two or -three.

Will didn't even leave while Chuck was changing, and Chuck had to smother both irritation and an urge to laugh at the heavy-handed attempt at intimidation. He simply stripped and changed, then followed Will back outside.

"We use racing school cars for this—they're former Cup cars that have been adapted with a second seat for passengers," the more reasonable Bart explained. "To get in—"

"I've got it," Chuck interrupted. There was only so much patronizing even he could stomach. "I've been to your races." While climbing in a car with no doors, however, Chuck understood why most drivers were smaller. Still, he managed fairly well.

For an old guy. Too bad he wasn't smiling at that anymore.

Bart got in his side, and they both strapped in. Will leaned into the passenger window and checked Chuck's fastenings.

Wouldn't want to kill him, he guessed. Not very good for their careers.

Then they were off, and if Chuck had ever possessed any tender sensibilities, it was obvious Bart wasn't going to spare them. Instead, he took off like a rocket, and it was like nothing Chuck had ever experienced. The closest he could come was flight school, but the G-forces seemed greater as they spun around the track, quickly reaching 7500 rpm, which Chuck guessed equated to 170 mph or so.

If he'd ever had a tendency toward motion sickness, he would have embarrassed himself for sure. Exactly what Bart and his brother were hoping for, that he'd get sick or beg them to slow down or something.

But they didn't know who they were messing with.

Instead, Chuck was grinning. "This is fantastic," he couldn't help saying, despite his resolve to stay silent. "I have got to drive one of these babies someday." He turned his head to see if Bart would offer.

Bart only sped up.

Chuck lost count of the laps, but finally a new voice came over the headphones. "Bart, we didn't refuel before you headed out."

"One more," Bart responded, and hit the gas.

"No, buddy. Pay attention. Time to come in."

But Bart, the one Maeve said was level-headed, ignored his crew chief and shot past the entrance to pit road.

Chuck had no shield on his helmet, so he knew that if Bart was looking, he'd see him smile. But he also had sons of his own and understood the demands of male pride, so he wiped any emotion from his face and kept quiet until at last, Bart pulled into his slot.

They sat there for a moment before unbuckling. "I'd do exactly the same in your place," Chuck said. "But what you don't understand is that I love your mother."

Bart's head whipped toward him, and he flipped up his visor, his eyes hot. "Then why would you do that to her last night? I don't think she slept for a second." Then, probably out of loyalty, Bart clamped his mouth shut.

"Is there somewhere we can talk in private, you, me and Will? It's not fair to her to do this in public."

Will approached his side and nodded with clear reluctance. "Let's go to my place."

The three of them crossed the garage area to the drivers' and owners' lot. Not a word was exchanged until they were inside Will's motor home.

Chuck spoke first. "You may not like to hear this, but your father's a first-class bastard. If I could get my hands on him and do some payback for what he's done to your mother, I'd be on him like white on rice."

"You'd have to stand in line," Will responded. Bart nodded agreement.

"Good. We're in accord on that." He glanced around, calculating his gamble. "Is there anything to drink here? I don't know how you two do this for a whole race. I'm dying of thirst."

Hearing that pleased them, he could tell. There was a time to strut your manly stuff, and there was a time to let others have what they needed. He'd risen to their challenge, but if things worked out, they would be his family, and a good father didn't humiliate his sons.

"Here." Will handed him a chilled bottle of water.

Chuck drank it halfway down before pausing. "People have no clue what hard work that is—and I was only riding."

Another point in his favor, he could see. But he meant it. "Listen, I'm not prepared to discuss everything that's happened between Maeve and me, because to do so would embarrass her. Some of it is too private for sons to hear." At their squirms, he smiled. "Yeah. Too much information." Then he sobered. "But the mistakes I've made were not intentional. I would not hurt your mother for the world. It's just that we don't know each other well enough yet, and women, well—" he shrugged "—does any man ever truly understand the way a woman thinks?"

"No one who's not kidding himself," Bart replied. When they both chuckled, Chuck was encouraged.

"I can tell you the nature of my mistakes, though,

if not the specifics." He'd had the whole night to ponder this. "I held back some truth from her because I thought it was for her own good." They shook their heads. "Yeah. Big mistake. But the other one, just as bad, was in trying to arrange things for her that I thought she needed. Trying to make life easier for her, to solve the problems I could."

"She's got a lot of them, doesn't she?" Will asked. "She won't discuss much with us."

"She does," Chuck concurred, "some that are serious, thanks to your dad—"

"Hilton," Bart corrected. "I want to forget he has any relation to me."

Will nodded grimly.

Chuck diverted from what he'd intended to say next. "I understand why you feel that way." He stepped down this path gingerly. "I'd be tempted, in your shoes." He hesitated, then plunged ahead. "I'm not saying you shouldn't, but I'd like to offer a little advice on that score. Hilton Branch is a selfish bastard nobody will disagree—but he's still half your gene pool."

"That's what makes me sick," Will muttered, and at that moment he was more boy than man.

"I'm not saying who he is has anything to do with who you are. I honestly don't believe that, Will. Your mother had far more to do with how you turned out." Both of them were paying full attention now. "But in the end, the men you become is all up to you." He pushed on. "Hating him will only warp you, and you're both better than that. Stronger than that. You'll give him too much importance if you focus on him, and what you need to do, just as your mother's trying to do, is move on. You may not like to hear this, but the best way to do that is to forgive him."

"What?" Will leapt to his feet. "No way. Do you know what he's done?" He started pacing, and even the calmer Bart looked agitated. "You have no idea what you're asking."

"I absolutely do." Will's head whipped around as Chuck said that. "My father abandoned my mother and me when I was a baby. Life was damn hard on her, with no education, no job skills, so young and still with a baby. She worked herself to death, is basically what happened. I started working young and did all I could to ease her burdens, but it was never enough, and she died before all my hard work paid off. So the bastard robbed me not only of a father but a mother, too." He heard the emotion he hadn't let himself feel in a long time. "I let myself hate him for too long, and it wasn't until I had sons of my own that I realized that it was robbing me—and worse, my family—of what we could have together. Taking up too much of the attention my children deserved."

He looked from one to the other. "Nobody learns from someone else's lesson, I know that. But just…think it over. For your mother's sake, if nothing else."

The two were silent for a long time. Finally Bart spoke. "So what are your intentions regarding Mom?"

"I never expected to want to say this again after losing my wife, but—" Chuck sucked in a deep breath "—if I can ever manage to get her to speak to me again, I want to marry her. How's that for the impossible dream?"

He grinned, and they grinned back. "Mom doesn't hold grudges," Will finally said. "But she's really hurt."

"I know, and I'm more sorry than you can imagine. So…any suggestions?"

"Man," Bart said, raking his fingers through his hair. "I have no idea how to get a woman to marry you. I spend too much time trying to prevent my girlfriends from thinking that far."

Chuck burst out laughing. "I don't know which problem's worse."

Bart grinned, and Will mirrored him. "Me, neither. Glad it's you and not me." Then he approached Chuck with his hand stuck out. "I was rude as hell earlier. Sorry."

Chuck shook his hand, then Bart's. "I don't blame you one bit. Maeve's fortunate to have such great kids. I'm lucky that way myself. Thanks."

"Do they know about Mom?" Bart asked. "Your kids?"

"No. They live far away, and, well…it's not like the woman hasn't given me mixed messages."

"You poor sap," Will said.

"Yeah," Chuck agreed. "Love can sure mess you up." Then he smiled. "But your mother is really something special."

"She is," replied Bart. "So what's next?"

"Beats the hell out of me," Chuck responded. He glanced at his watch. "Are we done here?" He met their eyes steadily.

"Yeah, we're done." Bart slapped him on the shoulder. "You did good out there."

"Thanks," Chuck said. "But I wasn't kidding about wanting to drive one."

Both faces beamed approval. "Get things squared with Mom, and you're on."

Chuck smiled. "I'll wait until one of you wins the championship."

"Better bet on me," Will boasted.

Bart punched his brother's arm. "He's a sap, not a sucker." With mutual backslaps, they started toward the door. "See you at the race?" Bart asked.

"With or without your mother." Chuck nodded.

"I'm hoping for with," Will said.

Chuck smiled after them. That was as close to a son's blessing as he was likely to get.

BARELY AN HOUR later, Chuck was in the middle of giving his assistant instructions on a counteroffer for a piece of land he had in mind to buy when his cell phone rang. "Hello?"

"Chuck, it's Will. I just got a call from Gerty. We can't leave here, but we need your help."

"Just a second, Will." He looked at his assistant. "Could you give me a second?"

She nodded and left, closing the door behind her.

"What's up?" he asked Will.

"Mom's headed for the jail to see Hilton. I don't think she should be alone."

Chuck stood up. Began to pace. She wouldn't welcome him, but that didn't matter. "When did she leave?"

"She just pulled out of the driveway, Gerty said."

He glanced at his watch. "My office is closer. I should be able to beat her there."

"Good. I wish one of us could go, but—"

"I'll take care of her, I promise." He grabbed his jacket and headed out the door.

"Thanks. Man, I have a bad feeling about this."

"Your mother is stronger than she knows, Will. Maybe stronger than any of us realizes."

"I hope you're right. Damn, I want to be there. I'd like to kick his ass."

"I hear you."

"I'm thinking about what you said, though. It's just—"

Chuck mouthed to his assistant that he'd be back and loped down the hall to the elevator. "You have to figure out your own path, son."

"Yeah. Anyway, thanks. Call if you need us. Mom's more important than anything else."

Chuck tapped his foot, waiting for the elevator. "Maeve wouldn't agree. She'd want you focusing on the race."

"She would. That's why she's so great. But this really is more important."

"You can count on me, Will. I promise."

A minute later Chuck was in the garage and sprinting to his car. He jumped in and hit the gas.

CHAPTER SEVENTEEN

MAEVE HAD NEVER BEEN near the jail complex before, and she'd nearly missed the turnoff. She'd almost lost her nerve and gone back home a hundred times on this trip, but she had to do this. She'd taken the easy way out too often.

Limited visiting hours meant a very crowded parking lot. After circling for eons looking for a space, at last she found one. As she crossed the expanse of pavement, she tried on one opening gambit after another. The polite one. *How are you, Hilton?* Outrage. *How could you do this to your children?* Hurt. *How could you do this to me?* Or, *I hate you—*

No. Hate was not an emotion Maeve wanted to dwell on. If she started, she might never stop.

Why? That was the question she really wanted to ask.

Even though she wasn't sure she could bear the answer.

"Maeve."

Lost in her thoughts, she jolted badly at the sound of her name. She looked up.

And thought her heart might stop.

"Chuck." She tried for neutrality. She failed. "What are you doing here?" Her eyes narrowed. "Gerty."

"She cares about you. She's worried, and so am I."

"I asked you to leave me alone."

He nodded, and his gray eyes locked on hers. "I made a big mistake, but I never meant to harm you. And you're wrong, that night we shared was not a mistake. We—"

She recoiled. "I can't talk about that night, not here." Then she recalled Cecily. Alyssa. "I can't talk to you, ever. We have nothing to discuss." She turned away.

He grabbed her arm. "Wait!"

She tried to shake him off, but he wouldn't release her, his hold gentle but resolute. "Listen to me, Maeve. Please."

She glanced up and saw her suffering mirrored in his eyes. She quit resisting.

"This isn't the time," he said, "and it's not why I'm here. Let me go in there with you. I think it's brave as hell of you to confront Hilton, but you don't have to do it alone."

"No."

"Maeve, please…" Then, to her surprise, he subsided. "I said you were brave, and I meant every word." He paused, drew a deep breath. "I don't like letting you face him alone, but I respect what you're doing. I'll be waiting when you're done."

She wondered if he could possibly understand what that meant. She was terrified, but she had to do this or she would never respect herself again. "There's no need."

"There's every need. I want you to lay the past to rest, because I intend to build a future with you."

"What?" She stared at him. "After last night? You have Cecily and…" She couldn't say the name. "I'm done with men who lie to me, men who don't find me enough, who want to direct my every move. Don't wait for me, Chuck. That night we had was a mistake, and it won't be repeated."

He stepped in front of her. "Cecily is a friend, only a friend, and you're delusional if you think Alyssa Ritchie could possibly appeal to me. Don't you use them as a crutch to dodge me, Maeve, don't you dare." He bent to her. "We are not done, I promise you that, sweetheart. Not by a long shot." He cupped her cheek, and the tenderness in his gaze nearly undid her. "But that's for later. For now, you go do what you have to do, and don't even try to give me the slip when you're finished." His eyes were intense. "I never give up on anything I really want, my love." But he only kissed her cheek. "And I want you more than I've ever wanted anything in my life."

One more caress, and he stepped aside, a muscle in his jaw flexing. "Go get 'em, Miss Maeve."

She stared at him in utter confusion but somehow turned away. Managed to cross the distance to the front door, glancing back at him twice.

The only good thing was that Chuck had her in such turmoil that before she knew it, she was through security and being ushered into a room where she was told Hilton would soon arrive.

When he did, she was shocked. The man she saw didn't resemble the man who'd disappeared in February. Photos she'd seen in the papers hadn't prepared her for the change in his appearance. Hilton Branch, larger than life, always with the flamboyant gesture, was nowhere in evidence.

The man across from her seemed...small. Too small to have wreaked such havoc, to have laid waste to so many lives. He'd lost weight, and his usual tan had faded to an alarming pallor. She was too stunned to speak.

"I was very surprised when they told me you were here, Maeve. I...I guess 'I'm sorry' doesn't do much," Hilton said. "But I am. I..." He glanced away, then began to talk, to catalog his misdeeds, to walk her through a litany of his decisions.

Maeve heard little of it, too shocked at first and then too angry. Her emotions seesawed. How could he possibly think an apology would ever be enough when he'd devastated all of them? Made a fool of her for the twenty years he'd had a mistress? Stolen her children's heritage? Robbed them all of the family home she was certain they'd lose?

Rage rolled over her in waves, rendering her deaf to his words until, in a stunning moment of clarity, she realized that nothing Hilton could say really mattered. That he was a weak, selfish man who, in the end, had engineered his own downfall and would pay dearly for his greed.

She would pay, too, as would their children, but her children had already climbed back to their feet, and she was doing so herself, if not quite so adroitly.

In the end, Hilton would lose everything—money, yes, and power and fame, all of which would devastate him—but he'd lost the most important thing long ago, whether he realized it or not. His family. His life could have been rich with love, but instead, he'd prized money more than any of them. She could be blamed for her own fate because she'd chosen badly and had compounded her error by putting on blinders to his behavior.

Her children, though, had done nothing but be amazing people, people Hilton had never seen for who they really were. They'd been status symbols to him, Penny with her face splashed on magazine covers, the twins rocketing to fame. Only Sawyer, who'd steadfastly refused to fall in line with his father's plans, had escaped the glare of Hilton's ambitions.

None of them deserved a father who couldn't really love them, and it was his loss.

His loss. She tuned back in to Hilton then, but this time, fury gave way to...pity. Pity—oh, how that would burn him, worse than anger ever could. And in that moment, Maeve knew that she was done with Hilton Branch, that he'd lost the power to hurt her.

That she'd been punished for her mistakes, but had also learned that she was strong enough to deal with whatever came next.

Whatever that life might be, she would be a different Maeve from the woman who'd sought refuge from the real world. The real world had come knocking on her door, anyway.

And the new Maeve would handle it.

Suddenly she was more than ready to be done with this chapter. She held up her hand to stop him. "I forgive you, Hilton."

His eyes widened in shock. "What?"

She stood to go. "I forgive you."

"But I haven't finished. Don't you want to—"

"No." She shook her head. "I've spent too much time going over the past and trying to understand, but you know what, Hilton? It doesn't matter what happened before. What's done is done. I'm moving on."

He blinked. "What's gotten into you, Maeve? You're not yourself."

She found herself smiling. "Actually, Hilton, I am. I'm just not the woman you married. Thank God." She turned to go. "Goodbye."

"But, Maeve," he spluttered, "we're not finished."

"Oh, yes, we most definitely are." She made the most satisfying exit of her life.

She returned through the halls, dizzy, unable to believe what she'd done. Barely seeing where she was going. She pressed her fingers to her forehead and tried to sort out what she was feeling. Free. Light. Unsettled and uncertain, but…

Free. The future yawned before her, but for the first time, she could see something besides darkness.

"Maeve."

And there he was, Chuck. So tall and strong and solid. Arms opening in welcome, a safe harbor.

She hesitated, struggling to know how to react. She still had a lot to figure out. "Chuck, I—"

"Shh. Give yourself a second." His voice, so deep and warm. So full of promise and comfort.

She let herself lean into him. His arms closed around her, and she exhaled, suddenly so weary she wasn't sure she could move.

He held her, and he rocked her slowly. He let her just…be.

The solace was a blanket of cashmere on a chilly night, a ray of sunshine on a dark day. With everything in her she yearned to snuggle inside his arms and never leave.

But he had deceived her. Didn't trust her.

Abruptly she lifted her head, ready to pull away.

Chuck kissed her—and every second of it was bliss.

He ended the kiss, but before she could figure what to say, he spoke. "I'm proud of you." Simple words that were like the finest champagne going straight to her head. "I was wrong." Then more words she had never heard Hilton say. "I wanted to wrap you in silk and tuck you away somewhere safe, but that wasn't fair, however well-meant. You've made huge strides in getting back on your feet, and I'm not being helpful when I try to protect you—it only holds you back. Not that I won't pitch in with whatever you need, be clear on that. But it's your call. Ask, and you've got it, whatever it might be." He brushed her hair away from her cheek. "I have faith in you. You're an amazing woman, Maeve."

He walked with her to her car, and when they reached it, he plucked the keys from her hand and opened the door, then saw her inside. "The next move is yours." With a last quick kiss, he left her there.

Maeve sat there, stunned. No idea what to say, what to do next. He'd just given her what she'd said she wanted, so why didn't she feel more jubilant?

She turned her head and spotted him getting into his car, and something inside her tore loose. A very good man was walking away from her, just as she'd asked. Making it clear that he believed her capable of handling her own life without interference.

Demonstrating more faith in her than anyone in her entire life ever had.

He couldn't be less like Hilton.

So was she going to just let him go? When she could still taste his kiss on her lips and knew what she was giving up, just to hang on to her pride?

Hadn't she wanted a man who appreciated her as she was, no artifice, no illusions? No secrets to hide?

Hadn't she wished for someone strong enough,

secure enough to let her flex her own muscles, yet one who'd stand behind her if she asked?

So what was she waiting for?

His car had backed out and was headed down the same row she was in. With a heart full of hope taking up all the room in her chest, Maeve leaped from her car and raced into the lane, planting herself in his path.

Chuck slammed on the brakes and jumped out of the car, his handsome features concerned. "Are you okay?"

"No." She shook her head. "But I will be." Then she tossed aside every last trace of proper composure and raced to him, leaping into his arms and planting, if she did say so herself, one very fine kiss on his lips.

He wasted not one instant deepening the embrace until they both finally had to come up for air.

"I call the shots, right?" she asked.

He nodded.

She laughed. "You won't always mean it."

"I will, Maeve, I swear I will." His grin turned sheepish. "Well, I promise to try."

She couldn't seem to stop smiling. "Thank you for what you said. About being proud of me."

"I am, sweetheart, you have no idea how proud I am. You took on Alyssa last night, and today, your expression tells me you took on Hilton just as successfully."

"I did, I really did." She nodded her head. "He wanted to explain everything, but I decided I didn't have to listen if I didn't want to. It was more important to be done with him."

"And you are?"

"Oh, yes. I told him I forgave him. Shocked him speechless."

"I bet."

"Then when he wanted to talk more, I just said no."

Chuck squeezed her. "That's my girl." Then he sobered. "I've got some explanations of my own to give."

She pressed a finger to his lips. "Not really. I think I understand. My reactions had more to do with my fears than the reality of how you've treated me."

"I shouldn't have sent Howard to you. Or given him the information. I should have told you it was my cabin."

"You're right, but I know you didn't do either one to hurt me."

He took her hand, brought it to his lips. "So... are you?"

"Am I what?"

"Are you my girl?" When she hesitated, he shook his head quickly. "No, that's not what I really want to ask. What I want to ask is this—will you marry me, Maeve?" At her shocked gasp, he plowed ahead. "I know the divorce isn't final, I know you've got lots else on your mind, so you don't have to answer right this second as long as you'll agree to marry me when the time is right." He flashed a devastating smile.

"But in the meantime, will you live with me in sin?" He waggled his eyebrows.

She found herself blushing. "I don't think—"

He rushed right over her objections. "If I don't get to take you to bed very soon, sweetheart, I won't be held accountable for the consequences." Then his gaze grew serious. "I've missed you every second since you left."

She couldn't seem to catch her breath. She used the moment to her advantage and let him suffer—just a little. "I was going to say that I don't think I want to wait until I get all my problems sorted out before I marry you—but you might not want to be dealing with them."

"Maeve." His voice was stern. "I'd have swept them all away long before now if you'd let me." Then his eyes lit. "You will? You'll marry me?"

"No. Yes. I mean, no, you won't sweep all my problems away, but if you'll bear with me while I do, that's enough. And yes, I'll marry you." She cast him a saucy leer. "Living in sin might shock our children."

"Well, we couldn't have that, now could we?" He picked her up and whirled her around and around in the parking lot until a driver wanting out honked several times loudly.

"Hold your horses!" Chuck shouted, then looked down at her. "I don't want to let you go. Come with me, and I'll send someone for your car."

She was still breathless from their laughter. "All right. Where are we going?"

"We're at the wrong courthouse. We have to go downtown to get our license."

"Just like that?"

More honking. Chuck shot the guy a glare.

Then looked back at her with the world in his eyes. "Unless you have a better plan."

"There's the small matter of my divorce."

"Well, damn." But he grinned. Swept her up into the passenger seat of his car. "Then our children are just going to have to get over the shock."

To the music of honking horns, they drove off.

Laughing again.

Feeling young and excited about the future.

* * * * *

For more thrill-a-minute romances set against
the exciting backdrop of the NASCAR world,
don't miss

VICTORY LANE by Marisa Carroll.
Available in December.

For a sneak peek, just turn the page!

"I'LL DRIVE YOU HOME, Patsy," he said. "Just like I used to all those years ago."

She didn't play coy or pretend she didn't understand the ramifications of getting into the car with him. "Oh, Dean, I don't think—"

He leaned down and kissed her, softly but thoroughly. "Shh," he said against her lips. "You think too much. C'mon, I've got a better idea. The truck's right over here. We'll take that instead. I'll just drive you out along the lake and we'll lie in the back and look up at the stars."

She laughed. She couldn't help herself. "Oh, no, you don't. In the first place, it's November and it's cold. And in the second place, every other time you tried that line on me we ended up doing all kinds of things but watch the stars."

"I know," he said in that low, sexy growl he reserved only for their lovemaking. "I remember each and every time, too." He plucked the keys from her nerveless fingers and pulled her into his arms, leaning back against her car. "Do you want me to describe them to you? The first time? The time the sheriff almost caught us in the act?" His voice deepened, darkened. "Or the time we made Sophia. I'll never forget that night." He was nuzzling her neck, molding her to him, and it felt so good. So very good.

Oh, God, she would never forget those magical nights either. Never. But they were long in the past. They were older now. Life wasn't all in front of them, a wonderful challenge. She was afraid now to look too far into the future. "I don't think that's a very good idea," she managed in what she hoped wasn't too breathless a tone.

He frowned a moment, then set her away from him, took her hand and started walking through the nearly empty parking area beside the Cargill hangar toward his truck. "Okay. We won't talk about memories of what we did years ago. We'll go to the farm and we'll make some new ones tonight."

She tried to muster her resolve to tell him no, but she couldn't. She seemed momentarily to have lost the hurt and the fear that had driven her these past few months. His hand was warm and strong in hers. It felt right to have him walking beside her, the other half of her she'd missed so badly. Didn't what they had shared together for so long deserve another chance?

He found his pickup, opened the passenger door and lifted her up onto the seat as though she was still the willowy sixteen-year-old she'd once been. She laid her head against the backrest of the passenger seat and closed her eyes. What was she doing? she asked herself, making one more attempt to deal logically with a purely emotional situation. How had she let herself be manipulated this way? The answer was simple and came readily to mind. *Because she still loved him.* Her heart raced in her chest. Heaven help her, she was still so very much in love with him.

Dean started the big truck and put it into gear. He was so close, the heat from his thigh brushing against hers as he turned a corner burned through her clothing. With one hand on the wheel, his arm draped across the back of the seat, he moved them out into the sparse, late-night traffic and turned, heading toward Concord.

They were on their way to the farm. They were on their way home.

A wave of exhaustion washed over her. She fought the sleepiness for a moment, then decided to give in to it, but not before she'd made her position plain to the man beside her. "Just because I'm letting you come home with me doesn't mean things are settled between us. It's just that tonight's a very important night for you."

"For us," he said, still in that private sexy growl. A shiver ran over her skin and she rubbed her hand up her arm to ease the prickling before it could move deeper into her body, turn into desire and take away her resolve.

"For us," she agreed, looking straight ahead. "I've missed you. I've missed making love to you. But I haven't changed my mind about anything. If you aren't going to retire from racing, then in the morning you'll have to leave. I may not be strong enough to get out of this truck and walk away from you right now, but I will be tomorrow."

//// *NASCAR*

Ken Casper
SCANDALS AND SECRETS

Tara Dalton is determined to interview Adam Sanford for her new racing biography. But he refuses to have *anything* to do with the project. Sanford Racing is Adam's life. But as Adam grudgingly lets her into the NASCAR world, he realizes he may have made a big mistake—falling for a woman who could ruin both his family and his reputation....

Feel the RUSH on and off the track.

Available February.

Visit www.GetYourHeartRacing.com
for all the latest details.

Love Inspired
SUSPENSE
RIVETING INSPIRATIONAL ROMANCE

WITHOUT A TRACE

Without a Trace: Will a young mother's disappearance
bring a bayou town together...or tear it apart?

WHAT SARAH SAW
by MARGARET DALEY
January 2009

FRAMED!
by ROBIN CAROLL
February 2009

COLD CASE MURDER
by SHIRLEE MCCOY
March 2009

CLOUD OF SUSPICION
by PATRICIA DAVIDS
April 2009

DEADLY COMPETITION
by ROXANNE RUSTAND
May 2009

Available wherever books are sold,
including most bookstores, supermarkets,
drugstores and discount stores.

Steeple
Hill®

www.SteepleHill.com

LISWATLIST